FROM TH[E] ...
OF MURDER

Mike James

TRUE
CRIME
LIBRARY

True Crime Library
A Forum Press Book
by the Paperback Division of
Forum Design,
PO Box 158, London SE20 7QA

An Imprint of True Crime Library
© 1996 Mike James
All rights reserved

Printed and bound by
Caledonian Book Manufacturing, Bishopbriggs,
Glasgow G64 2QR

ISBN 1 874358 18 4

CONTENTS

PREFACE

A housewife dreams her mother has been murdered. Unable to rest, she drives over to check. Her mother is fine. But within minutes of the daughter's arrival the old lady is dead.

Nobody can explain the paranormal, but its reality is beyond dispute — like the above incident, which with many more of its kind is detailed in the following pages: bizarre events which read like fiction but happen to be fact.

There's no disputing them because they were coolly and clinically recorded when they occurred. They had to be, because in most instances they had sequels in court, at murder trials or inquests.

The people who noted the details were not psychic researchers predisposed to believe in the supernatural. They were down-to-earth policemen, lawyers and reporters. People just doing their job and inclined to be sceptical. Yet what they chronicled was beyond rational explanation.

How was a medium able to identify the rendezvous of two killers simply by handling the victim's belongings? Nobody knows, but the spiritualist's tip helped to send two men to the gallows.

How could a pint-sized weakling overpower two six-foot musclemen, tossing the body of one into a river? Detectives couldn't believe he'd acted alone until they saw him demonstrate his superhuman strength. Everything about him defied explanation ... including the way he went to his execution.

How did a London clergyman's wife know that her son lay dead at the bottom of a well? She dreamt it, and detectives found she was right. How did a schoolgirl know that her family would never return from the sailing trip they were to make to the Bahamas, as she told her teacher and classmates? She too was right. They were murdered.

Why did Scotland Yard's Robert Fabian have to make a study of witchcraft? Why were Detroit's detectives baffled by the multiple killer their chief described as "a murderer from the Dark Ages"? The investigators were probing cases which involved the occult.

Similarly, the part played by coincidence in the annals of crime takes some believing. Like the story behind a razor found on a London bus, an incident which a police superintendent recalled as the weirdest in his long career.

Such cases in the X Files keep us guessing to this day. Incidents so incredible that some people have flatly refused to believe them, despite irrefutable evidence. It was so when two children from nowhere perished in a Gloucestershire train crash. Nobody knew who they were. Nobody claimed them, and there were those who insisted the pair never existed. But their gravestone serves as mute testimony to the truth of their story.

It seemed that their deaths had been more than convenient to someone, and the railway disaster itself had more than an element of mystery. Had somebody targeted a whole train-load of passengers just to get rid of two?

Quite the last place where you might expect to encounter the paranormal is within the austere four walls of a court, but such settings are not immune to the supernatural, as the X Files show. Read on and you'll find a witness having his memory jogged by someone from the spirit world at a murder trial in Winchester.

The X Files, as you will have gathered, are the repository for inexplicable cases that can't be pigeonholed anywhere else. Cases that tease the imagination, stories that challenge all logic. We can only accept them, just as Simon Fraser had to accept the court order which compelled him to sleep alone, locked in a bedroom at his Glasgow home. Why that order was imposed is another X Files story told in these pages. Turn them, and you enter the world of the unknown ...

1
SUPERMAN'S NIGHTMARE
CHICAGO, AUTUMN, 1921

Superman is just fantasy ... isn't he? In 1921, Chicago detectives weren't so sure. The man before them defied rational explanation. They couldn't believe his claims ... until he demonstrated them before their startled eyes. And right up to his last gasp he continued to astonish them.

But he was a superman gone wrong. Something had warped him. He'd become a ruthless killer.

The first body was found by ten-year-old Edward Baker. It was autumn, 1921, and with another boy he was playing on the Lake Street bridge that crosses the Desplaines River at Maywood, a suburb of Chicago. Suddenly he pointed to something in the river.

"Look!" he shrilled excitedly. "There goes a dead body! That's how they float when they're dead — face down in the water."

The other boy climbed on the rail beside him, and they stared down at the muddy current. The gruesome object, unquestionably the body of a dead man, floated slowly down the river and passed beneath the bridge.

"We'd better find a policeman," decided Edward, and ran down the street, his companion pounding after him. Two blocks away they found a Maywood police officer and breathlessly told him what they had seen.

The officer hurried to the bank of the river, untied a canoe and paddled downstream after the dead man's body. He drew alongside it, fastened a rope around its neck and towed it back to the bank.

As he dragged the body from the water, he saw that the man's face was almost obliterated. His skull was crushed, his throat slit, his features bruised and battered.

Then he saw something else. The man's legs were tied together with rope and his wrists were locked behind his back with handcuffs!

When the body was taken to the Maywood morgue it was established that the motive for the murder was not robbery. In the dead man's pockets the police found $27 in cash and an expensive gold watch.

The fractured skull and broken neck, the blows rained on the man's face, presumably after he was tied and handcuffed, indicated that he had been tortured.

Papers found on the body identified it as that of Bernard J. Daugherty of 618 Oakdale Street, Chicago. The Maywood police called Chicago police headquarters, and Lieutenant John Norton answered the phone.

"Bernard J. Daugherty?" Norton repeated. "There are two men in my office right now asking about a Bernard J. Daugherty. They say he's been missing since yesterday noon. We'll come out and have a look at the body."

Lieutenant Norton and his squad arrived at the Maywood morgue with two men from the Packard Motor Sales Company of Chicago.

The Packard men looked at the disfigured corpse on the slab, examined the papers found on it and told the police it was Bernard Daugherty, employed by their company as a salesman.

The day before, they said, he and Carl Ausmus, another salesman, had left the Packard salesroom with a customer who had bought a $5400 car. Since then no word had been received from either.

"So Ausmus is missing too," commented Lieutenant Norton. "Who is this person who bought the car, and where does he live?"

His name, they told him, was Harvey Church. His address, 2922 Fulton Street.

At this point Peter M. Hoffman, coroner of Cook County, arrived and examined the body.

"Look at the build of this man," he said. "More than six feet tall and weighing over 200 pounds. I can see he was a man of tremendous muscular force and probably in the pink of physical condition."

The Packard officials corroborated this. Daugherty, they told the coroner, had been a college athlete before joining their sales force and was noted for his enormous strength.

"Then it would surely take more than one man," the coroner continued, "to overpower him, handcuff his wrists behind his back, tie his legs and beat him to death."

While a detective sergeant untied the rope from the victim's legs and tackled the handcuffs with a file, the coroner and Lieutenant Norton questioned the Packard officials, who said that Daugherty had come from Boston to join the Chicago sales force. Later the company had employed Carl Ausmus of Bloomington, Illinois. Both became good salesmen.

About a week before, a young man had called at the Packard salesroom and selected a car priced at $5400. He said his name was Harvey Church. After a demonstration he bought the car and said he would return for it on Thursday and pay the full amount in cash. On Thursday morning he had called for the car.

He told the sales manager he had the money at the Madison-Kedzie Bank.

The car was turned over to him, and Daugherty and Ausmus were sent along to collect the money. The young man known as Church climbed in behind the wheel and drove the car. Daugherty sat in the front beside him. Ausmus sat in the back.

An hour later, as agreed, the manager sent Edward Skelba, a chauffeur, to the bank in another car to pick up the two salesmen and drive them back to the office. Skelba drove to the bank and waited outside in his car. There was no sign of either Daugherty or Ausmus. After waiting two hours, he went to a corner drugstore and called his office.

The sales manager told him to wait a while longer.

When Skelba returned to his car, which he had parked in front of the bank, he found a card tied to the steering wheel. It was Daugherty's business card and on the back of it was written: "Ed: Go back to the office. Will come in later.—B.J.D."

The card had been tied to the wheel while Skelba was in the drugstore, telephoning. It was after two o'clock by now and the bank was closed. Skelba went back to the Packard office.

"And from that moment to this," the Packard officials ended, "we've had no word from Ausmus. And now we find Daugherty lying here like this!"

"You say Ausmus is also a man of considerable strength?" asked Hoffman.

"He's about the same build as Daugherty and probably fully as strong."

"Then it may be," said the coroner, "that Ausmus murdered Daugherty in order to get the money that Church had paid him. You say Ausmus was in the army?"

"That's right."

"And those are army handcuffs," said Coroner Hoffman, pointing to the wrists of the murdered man. "Doesn't that seem significant?"

"It does," agreed one of the Packard men. "Still I can't picture Ausmus doing a thing like this."

"Getting back to this fellow Church," said Lieutenant Norton, "is he also powerfully built?"

"On the contrary," said the Packard man, "Church is an undersized chap and rather anaemic-looking. He probably weighs less than 130 pounds."

"That seems to let Church out," the coroner commented.

"Maybe it does and maybe it doesn't," said Lieutenant Norton. "Anyhow, we'll look up this Church and see what he has to say."

The handcuffs had been filed from the dead man's wrists and were given to two detectives, who started out to cover all army goods stores in the Chicago district. Lieutenant Norton took the piece of rope, and with Hoffman and the two Packard men set out for the home of Harvey Church. On the way they stopped at the Madison-Kedzie Bank and asked if Harvey Church had an account there.

He had, they were told, and until the previous morning he had a balance to his credit of $225.

"Yesterday morning," said one of the cashiers, "he checked out $200."

They drove on to Church's home. It was a two-flat building, none too prosperous looking, in a squalid neighbourhood. Young Church, they discovered, occupied the lower flat, living alone with his mother.

But neither he nor his mother was at home. The place was locked up and deserted.

The ringing of the doorbell and loud knocks on the door got no response from the lower flat, but it aroused the tenants in the flat above —

Gunnar W. Ekquist and his wife Bertha.

Mrs. Ekquist said, "I saw Harvey Church drive up here yesterday in a brand-new car. It was about one o'clock in the afternoon. I saw him get out of the car and go inside the house. I went on with my housework, and when I looked from the window again the car was gone."

"Did you notice anybody else in the car with him?" Norton asked.

"Yes, there were two men with him," said Mrs. Ekquist. "Big fellows, they were. One sat in the front seat, the other in the rear. They stayed in the car while Harvey went inside the house."

"Doesn't it seem strange to you," the detective asked the coroner, "that a young man living in this sort of house, in this kind of neighbourhood, would be buying a $5400 automobile?"

"It does seem strange," admitted Hoffman.

The lieutenant's suspicions strengthened when he learned from Mrs. Ekquist that Harvey Church was a railway brakeman, employed only occasionally by the Chicago & Northwestern Railway.

"There's something phoney here," he said. "I think we'd better search this place."

He and his men forced the flat open, and tramped inside. The blinds were drawn, the rooms half dark, and there was a musty odour. They were the sort of rooms you'd expect to find in the home of any young mechanic living with his mother in modest circumstances.

Then the men descended the steps that led from the kitchen to the basement. Opening the door they were struck speechless with horror.

The place was like a slaughter-house. Blood was spattered on everything — on the odds and ends of broken furniture, on the floor and even on the walls.

In one corner there lay a bloody baseball bat and beside it on the cement floor lay a bloodstained hammer and hatchet. Blood-soaked clothing and newspapers were scattered about in a gory mess which included two bloodstained hats, one bearing the initials "B.J.D." the other, "C.A." They were the hats of Bernard J. Daugherty and Carl Ausmus.

Equally significant was a short length of rope that Lieutenant Norton lifted from rubbish in another corner. He compared it with the piece of rope he had removed from the body of the murdered man. Both appeared to be from the same length.

Upstairs the investigators found a photograph of Harvey Church and some letters from Adams, Wisconsin, written by the young man's father.

Another neighbour, Mrs. Marguerite Gardiner who lived next door, provided a clue. "About five o'clock this morning," she said, "I was awakened by the sound of a car in the street, and when I looked outside I saw Harvey Church and his mother driving off in a swell new Packard."

"Did they look as if they were going very far?" Lieutenant Norton asked.

"Well, they had a lot of luggage in the car," said the woman, "so I guess they were going on a long trip."

Norton thought of the letters from Adams, Wisconsin. He called headquarters, and a telegram was sent to Joseph Paulsen, town marshal of Adams: *"Arrest and hold Harvey Church, son of Edwin O. Church, your city, wanted for murder in Chicago. Is probably driving new twin-six Packard; licence number Illinois, 449672. May be accompanied by mother."*

There followed a description of Harvey Church, as gathered from the photograph found in his home and information supplied by the neighbours.

Coroner Hoffman, however, still had his doubts. "Is it reasonable to believe," he argued, "that if Church murdered that man he would leave such a wide-open trail? He made no effort whatever to cover up his tracks."

Some of the detectives agreed. They believed that Church had paid Daugherty for the car and that Ausmus had murdered Daugherty in order to get possession of the money. The murder, they thought, had been committed in Church's basement, without his knowledge, and he had left with his mother in the car he had bought, unaware of anything wrong.

Another police theory was that Daugherty might have been killed in a violent quarrel over a woman. His mutilated body suggested the work of a man crazed with jealousy.

Detectives trying to discover where the handcuffs had been obtained finally traced them to the army goods store of Charles Izenstock. They dropped the rusty handcuffs on the counter, and beside them a photograph of Harvey Church.

"Did you sell those cuffs to that fellow?" they asked Mr. Izenstock.

"No," said Mr. Izenstock. "But perhaps my assistant did."

The assistant looked at the handcuffs and said, "Yes, I sold these just the other day for $2.95." Then he looked at the photograph and added: "That *looks* like the fellow who bought them, but I can't be sure."

Late that night, Lieutenant Norton received a phone call from town marshal Joseph Paulsen in Adams, Wisconsin.

Harvey Church had been found and was under arrest!

Paulsen had spotted a huge new twin-six Packard rolling down the main street of Adams. The young man at the wheel was clearly enjoying the envious stares of the other young men of the town. His attitude was that of a small-town boy who has made good in the big city and returned home to show off.

Sitting proudly in the front seat beside him was one of the local belles. In the back was an elderly woman.

Paulsen drove up behind the gleaming limousine and noted the number. It was Illinois 449672! The marshal swung alongside.

"Pull up to the kerb," he shouted to the youth at the wheel. "Your name Harvey Church?"

"Sure," replied the young man, surprised. "Why?"

The marshal flashed his badge and said: "You're under arrest. They want you in Chicago for murder."

Church looked incredulous. Then he laughed and called over his shoulder to the white-haired woman, "Did you hear that, Mother? They want me for murder! If that isn't a joke!"

But it was no joke to Joseph Paulsen. He took the young man to the lock-up and telephoned the Chicago police. Norton sent two of his best men to Adams to bring back the suspect. With them went A. M. Devoursney of the Burns Detective Agency, retained by the Packard company.

The young man greeted the detectives affably. His manner suggested he had nothing to fear. He seemed to regard the whole thing as a joke.

Nevertheless, he had retained two lawyers, and he insisted that both accompany him on his return trip to Chicago.

Edwin Church, his father, was well known and respected in Adams, and when the townsfolk heard the news they hurried to his home in consternation. He assured them there was nothing to worry about, saying, "The police have simply made a blunder."

Blunder or not, the three detectives bundled Harvey Church into the new Packard and started back to Chicago.

They allowed Harvey to drive the car, which he seemed to enjoy immensely, and they did their best to put him at ease and allay any suspicion he might have of the seriousness of the case against him.

They said nothing about the discovery of Daugherty's dead body; neither did they mention the matter of the handcuffs, nor the grisly scene found in his basement. If he knew of these things, they reasoned — and knew what a strong case they had against him — he might refuse to cross the state line into Illinois, which would mean a delay for extradition proceedings.

So they chatted with him amiably as he sent the high-powered car zooming along the Wisconsin highways. "This car, now," said Devoursney, "where did you get it?"

Church answered easily: "Where do you suppose I got it? I bought it, of course."

"You paid for it?"

"Naturally."

"Who did you pay?" asked Devoursney.

"The fellows I bought it from — a couple of Packard salesmen named Ausmus and Daugherty." Church, who had answered all their questions without hesitation, called to his mother in the back seat: "Isn't that right, Mother? Didn't I pay for this car?"

The woman nodded her head emphatically. "Of course you paid for it, Harvey. I saw you." Then she said to the detective sitting beside her: "My son has done nothing wrong. He has nothing to fear. That's why he's so willing to go back to Chicago with you."

The Burns detective sitting beside Church went on persuasively: "How did you pay the salesman,

Harvey — in cash or with a cheque?"

"I paid them with Liberty bonds," said Harvey Church. "There were nine bonds altogether — five of $1000 each and four of $100. Fifty-four hundred dollars."

"Did they give you a receipt?"

"Sure," said Church. He slowed the car and took a wallet from his pocket. He slipped a paper from the wallet and handed it to the detective. "There you are," he said.

Devoursney looked at the paper and saw at a glance it was no receipt but merely a customer's order for a car. He said nothing about this, however, but handed it back, remarking pleasantly: "Yes, everything seems to be in order."

Church smiled. "Sure, everything's in order. Why shouldn't it be? I bought this car and paid for it, and that's all there is to it. I don't know what's eating you men, but if there's anything wrong I'll do all I can to help you."

Beguiled by the detectives' friendly manner, Church was relaxed. But once they had crossed the state line and were in Illinois, their manner changed. One of them told their captive to move over, and slid behind the driver's wheel.

With Church wedged between him and the Burns detective, he drove the car into Chicago and to Detention Home No. 1. It was now three o'clock in the morning.

The Packard was left there, and Church and his mother were bundled into a police patrol wagon and driven to the Criminal Courts Building. There the suspect was led into the office of the State's Attorney for prolonged questioning.

Up to now, Church had been the life of the party, laughing and joking with all around him; but when he walked into the "inquisition room" of State's Attorney Robert E. Crowe, between two detectives, and saw the grim-faced interrogators awaiting him, his assurance seemed to waver.

The interview was started by Captain Mullen, and Assistant State's Attorney Charles Wharton.

"You say you gave those salesmen nine Liberty bonds?" Captain Mullen asked.

"That's right," said Church.

"Where were you when you gave them the bonds?"

"We were in the Crystal Restaurant, on Madison Street near Kedzie Avenue."

"When you gave them the bonds," said Wharton, "what did they give you?"

"They gave me seven keys for the car and a bill of sale," Church replied.

"Let's see it."

Church pulled out his wallet and handed over the same slip of paper he had shown to Detective Devoursney.

Captain Mullen looked at it, while the others gathered around and read it over his shoulder. He flipped it back to Church.

"That's no bill of sale," he said. "That's only a customer's order."

Church puckered his brows as if surprised. Then he began searching his wallet and pockets.

"I don't seem to have the other paper with me," he said. "I must have left it in my other suit of clothes. Anyway, I got a bill of sale."

"All right. We'll come back to that later," said Captain Mullen. "After you gave those bonds to the salesmen, where did you go with them?"

"I didn't go anywhere with them," Church answered. "The three of us left the restaurant and I climbed into the car, which we'd parked outside.

They walked down the street and I drove off alone."

"Did you see them again?"

"No, sir."

Chief Inspector Ben Newmark now took up the questioning. "You say you haven't seen either Ausmus or Daugherty since you left them outside the restaurant?"

"No, sir; I haven't seen them since that moment."

"Don't you know that we've found Daugherty's dead body?"

For the first time Harvey Church was visibly agitated. "My God, no! What happened to him?" he cried, clearly shocked.

"He was murdered," said the inspector. "His legs were roped together and his hands were fastened behind his back with handcuffs. His skull was crushed and his throat was slit, and his face had been hammered with a baseball bat."

"That is terrible!" gasped Church.

"But that isn't all we found," the inspector went on. "In the basement of your home we found the baseball bat that was used on Daugherty's skull. We also found Daugherty's hat and the hat that belonged to Carl Ausmus."

"But —"

"You murdered Daugherty!" Newmark thundered. "You murdered him with that baseball bat. You handcuffed his hands behind his back and tied his legs so he couldn't defend himself, and then you cut his throat and battered his head to a bleeding pulp ..."

Church leapt to his feet and was forced back into his chair.

"After you murdered Daugherty you murdered Ausmus. You dumped Daugherty's body into the Desplaines River. What did you do with the body of

Ausmus? Where have you hidden it?"

Church struggled against the restraint of the two officers who held him down in his chair. "I don't know what you're talking about!" he screamed angrily. "I didn't do it! You're crazy! If you think I did such a thing, you're all crazy as hell!"

The rusty handcuffs were jangled before his face.

"We know where you bought these," he was told. "You bought them at the army goods store of Charles Izenstock in South Clark Street."

Church screamed: "I didn't do it! I tell you, I didn't do it!"

The grilling continued for hours. The interrogators' voices carried into the outer corridor and into the adjoining office. And when Mrs. Church, seated outside, heard her son's protesting screams she fainted.

While she lay unconscious, and while her son was shrieking denials at the relentless ring surrounding him, another drama was being enacted at their home. Police were digging up the Church basement and back-yard in a search for the body of the missing Ausmus.

It was a pitch-black night. The flickering light of the police lanterns pushed back the wall of darkness. Finally, as dawn began to break, Sergeant John Hanrahan stood looking about the small yard in the half-light of the lanterns. He and his men had dug everywhere without finding anything.

He walked over to the garage and took another look inside. Here, too, the earth had been spaded up without any result.

His eyes came to rest on the ancient car that Church had abandoned when he acquired the new Packard.

Hanrahan's gaze narrowed on the car, and

suddenly he noticed something that made him step closer. He rested his lantern on the running-board and bent down for a look at the wheels. Then he straightened up and called to Sergeant Charles Welling.

"Have a look at this Charlie. Do you see anything unusual about it?"

Sergeant Welling looked at the car and shook his head.

"Look at the wheels on this side," Hanrahan said, "then at the wheels next to the wall. Those wheels are five or six inches lower than these. Let's push this thing out of here."

They rolled the car out of the garage, and then went back inside. Welling held the lantern while Hanrahan stooped and inspected the ground next to the wall. Around the tyre marks where the car had stood were freshly turned cinders!

Hanrahan seized a spade. Scraping the cinders aside, he saw a pair of man's shoes. Shovelling swiftly, he soon uncovered a man's body, buried face down just below the surface ...

The dead man's hands were tied behind his back with rope, which was also around his legs and ankles, binding them securely together.

The body was quickly identified as that of the missing Packard salesman, Carl Ausmus.

Like his colleague, Bernard Daugherty, he had been beaten with inhuman brutality. His neck was broken, his skull fractured, and his face battered until it was almost unrecognisable. But he had suffered an even more horrible death.

This was determined by physicians when they made their post-mortem examination. Ausmus, though beaten ferociously, with his hands tied behind him, was still alive when his murderer had flung him face down in a shallow grave and covered his body with cinders.

The killer had then jumped on the head of his prostrate victim — so the physicians believed — and ground his heels in the back of his neck, breaking it.

And as in the case of Daugherty, the motive for the murder had apparently not been robbery. Forty dollars was found in a wallet in the dead man's hip pocket. His other pockets contained some silver and a gold pencil. And he wore an army wrist watch, which had stopped at 6.48.

More discoveries were made when the body was taken to an undertaker's and the clothing removed. The victim had been tortured in a manner too shocking for the details to be printed.

But one fact can be mentioned. Coroner Peter Hoffman, standing beside the body, noticed a thread protruding from the swollen lips. He took the thread in his fingers and pulled on it. The thread snapped.

He forced the lips apart and saw cloth wadded inside the dead man's mouth. He tried to pull it out, but couldn't. Doctors had to make an incision before the cloth could be extracted. When they finally got it out they stared at it in disbelief.

It was a woman's brassière! It had been thrust far down the windpipe with gorilla-like strength.

Back at the Criminal Courts Building, in the office of State's Attorney Robert E. Crowe, interrogators were still sweating young Harvey Church — and still getting the same answer to all their questions: "I didn't do it!"

His thin body crumpled in the chair, his eyes darting wildly at his questioners. Try as they did — using every device known to the police for squeezing confessions from recalcitrant prisoners — the interrogators could get nothing more than that.

Then word came of the discovery of Ausmus's body and the questioning ended, momentarily.

The interrogators went into a huddle and agreed on a new strategy. Saying nothing to the prisoner about the discovery of the second body, they turned him over to Lieutenant John Norton.

"Come along, Church," Norton said. "We're going for a walk."

The frail young man got out of his chair, watching the detective warily. He was led from the room between two sergeants and placed in a squad car.

Norton drove him first to the Lake Street bridge at Maywood. They got out at the spot where 10-year-old Eddie Baker had seen the body of Daugherty floating in the river. Church was led to the rail and Lieutenant Norton directed his attention to the muddy water below. A pale grey mist hovered over the surface.

"That's where they found his body, Church," Lieutenant Norton said grimly. "It was tied and handcuffed — just as you slid it into the river."

Church averted his eyes. His face was pale and drawn in the morning light. "I didn't do it!" he whispered.

"Come on," said Norton, and led the way back to the car.

He drove next to the mortuary where the body of Daugherty had been taken. At that early hour the place was closed, but Norton unlocked the door and led his prisoner to a rear room where Daugherty's corpse lay on a slab.

Holding Church by the wrist, Norton jerked the sheet from the mutilated body.

"There he is, Church! There's the man you killed! Look at him! He can't hurt you now. He's dead. Confess that you killed him!"

Church staggered back and tried to cover his face. But he didn't confess.

"Come on," said Norton, and led him back to the car. Their next stop was the young man's home.

The detectives led him through the rooms of the lower flat and down the basement steps. Norton pointed to the bloodstains on the basement walls.

"Here is where you killed him, Church. You handcuffed his hands behind his back and crushed his skull with a baseball bat. You hammered his face and cut his throat. Then you threw his body into the river. Confess!"

Church flung one hand across his eyes and shook his head from side to side. "I didn't do it," he gasped.

Norton had saved his trump card. "Come on," he said. "I've something else to show you."

He dragged the suspect from the basement and across the small back yard and into the garage. He pointed at the freshly dug earth and cinders — at the spot where police had disinterred the body of Ausmus.

"Look, Church! Look at that grave! That's where you buried Carl Ausmus. He was still alive when you buried him. You threw him face down and stamped on his neck. You wanted to make sure he'd die. Confess!"

"I tell you I didn't do it!" Church's voice by now was scarcely more than a croak.

"Get down there," said Lieutenant Norton, "and show me how you buried him. He's dead now. He can't hurt you."

Church knelt beside the shallow grave. His eyes darted frantically. He licked his dry lips. Then he pitched forward on his face and lay still. He had fainted.

The sergeants picked him up and carried him out to the squad car. Norton drove him back to the Criminal Courts Building. He was taken again to the state's attorney's office.

The questioning was resumed where it had been broken off. But it showed no promise of getting anywhere, Church still protesting that he knew nothing about the two killings. The police and the coroner's office were still divided in their theories. The police believed Church had killed the two men, his motive being to get possession of the car without paying for it.

But Coroner Hoffman was convinced that more than one man was involved in the double murder, and there was logic to bear him out.

Assuming that Church had murdered the men for the car, would he have driven away in it without making any effort to cover his tracks? Would he have given his correct name and address to the Packard company? Would he have awakened his neighbour, Mrs. Marguerite Gardiner, on the morning he started for Adams, Wisconsin?

And if the motive for the murder was robbery, why hadn't he taken his victims' money and other valuables?

On top of all this, could any man of his frail build overpower two giants such as Ausmus and Daugherty, handcuff and tie them, and brutally batter them to death?

Some of the detectives were inclined to agree with Coroner Hoffman. They hadn't discarded the theory that the first murder, if not the second, had been committed by an enraged husband or a jealous rival in some affair.

Another notion was that the two Packard salesmen had been killed by a gang of car thieves, who had planted the evidence at Church's house in order to implicate him and throw the police off the scent. Working on this angle, squads of detectives rounded up a number of suspects and brought them in for questioning.

Meanwhile the interrogation of Church continued.

"Has somebody made you fall guy, Harvey?" asked Hoffman.

Church, near to collapse, answered hoarsely: "Yes. This thing is a frame-up. There are certain men who hate me. They framed me for those murders and want me to take the rap. They hate me because I scabbed in the switchmen's strike. They'd do anything to get me — even murder."

"Who are these men?" the coroner asked.

Church hesitated. Finally he said: "One of them is Leon Parks. He works in Gus Benario's garage at 2815 West Lake Street."

"Who are the others?"

"There's only one other. His name is Wilder, Clarence Wilder, but everybody calls him Bud. I'm not sure where he lives, but he works in a shoe factory."

Detectives found Parks without difficulty and brought him to the State's Attorney's office, while another squad was looking for Wilder.

Parks was a lean, hollow-cheeked young man, about Church's age. When he was brought into the room where Church was held, he seemed nervous and fearful of meeting Church's eyes.

Church, on the other hand, underwent a surprising change the moment Parks entered the room. He rose buoyantly from his chair as if a great load had been lifted from his shoulders. His eyes glittering, he looked at Parks and said sternly, "Look at me Leon!"

Leon Parks slowly lifted his gaze to meet Church's accusing eyes.

"Yes, Harvey?" he said meekly.

Church stepped nearer and looked Parks in the eye with a peculiar intensity.

"You killed those two men, didn't you, Leon?"

"What two men, Harvey?"

"You know what two men! Those two Packard salesmen, Ausmus and Daugherty. You and Bud Wilder killed them. You killed them in my basement. You thought you could pin the crime on me. Isn't that right?"

"B-but, Harvey …"

"Don't deny it!" Harvey Church thrust his face within an inch of Parks. "And don't try to avoid my eye. Look me squarely in the eye and tell me the truth. *Didn't you and Wilder kill those men?*"

Parks tried to shift his gaze, but he was impaled by Church's glittering eyes. He licked his dry lips and said in a wavering voice: "Yes, Harvey. We killed them."

Church looked around at the astonished officers. "Well, what did I tell you?" he said.

Scarcely able to believe what they had heard, they called in a stenographer.

Under a hail of questions from Church and the officers, Parks described in detail how he and Clarence Wilder had murdered the Packard salesmen and disposed of their bodies.

"We lured them into the basement," he said in response to a question from Church. "We got Daugherty first. We handcuffed his hands behind his back and killed him with a baseball bat. Then we got the other fellow and killed him the same way. We dumped one of the bodies in the river and buried the other in Harvey's garage."

Chief Inspector Ben Newmark asked: "But why did you want to kill them?"

Parks hesitated and looked at Church. Church looked him sternly in the eye and said:

"You killed them for the Liberty bonds you knew I'd given them. Isn't that right?"

"Yes, that's right, Harvey."

Parks's answers — most of them to questions asked by Church — detailed how the crime was committed. Typewritten copies of his confession were then given to him for his signature.

He had scarcely signed them before the door opened and detectives came in with Clarence "Bud" Wilder volubly protesting against his arrest.

"Is this the man who helped you with the murder?" Coroner Hoffman asked Parks.

Parks looked at the angry Wilder and said: "Yes; that's the man."

Wilder exploded. "You liar!" he shouted. "Look at my face! You never saw me before, and you know it!"

Inspector Newmark ended the ruckus by taking Wilder out to another room and questioning him privately.

"You mean to tell you don't even know that fellow in there?"

"I never saw him before in my life," said Wilder.

"How about the other fellow — Church?"

"I know him," said Wilder, "but this is the first time I've seen him in weeks. I first met him during the switchmen's strike a few months ago. We roomed together for a while."

"What can you tell me about those killings?"

"Only what I've read in the newspapers. That's all I know about them."

"What were you doing on Thursday, the day those men were killed?"

"On Thursday," said Wilder, "I was working all day at my job in the factory."

Newmark sent two detectives to the shoe factory where Wilder was employed, with orders to interview the foreman and other employees and check on the time clock for Thursday. Then leaving Wilder in the custody of two other detectives, he went back to the room where his brother officers were puzzling over Parks's confession.

He stood inside the doorway and looked at Parks and Church. There was something peculiar in the attitude of these two young men — and something still more peculiar in the confession that Parks had signed.

He whispered to a detective to get Church quietly out of the room. Then he walked over and sat down beside Parks.

"Look here, Parks," he said. "You said you and Wilder killed those men so that you could rob them. If that is so, how does it happen you didn't take their money and watches?"

Parks's eyes roamed the room as if seeking help.

Inspector Newmark, watching him closely, said, "Church isn't here to prompt you now. You're on your own. Speak up. Why did you and Wilder do it?"

Parks began to whimper. "We *didn't* do it."

"What!"

"I mean I — don't know why we did it. You'll have to ask Harvey."

"Look, Leon. You needn't be afraid of Harvey now. You can tell us the truth. Did you and Wilder kill those two men?"

Parks, verging on tears, vigorously shook his head. "No," he said, "we didn't. I don't know who killed them."

"Then why did you say you killed them?"

"I don't know. I don't know why I told you that, unless it was because Harvey wanted me to."

"My God!" exploded Newmark. "Do you mean to tell us you confessed a murder that you never committed merely because somebody wanted you to?"

"I was in a dream. I was there, I could see us getting them into the basement, Daugherty first. I knew it was a dream, but it wouldn't stop. We handcuffed him and whacked him with a baseball bat, but somehow I wasn't doing it, only it was a nightmare."

Parks was too confused to speak any more. He could only nod his head in agreement.

Newmark jumped up from his chair and strode across to the adjoining room where Church was sitting calmly in a chair, guarded by two detectives.

"What's the meaning of this?" he thundered. "What's the idea of that guy in there telling us that crazy crap story about dreaming he did those murders? He had nothing to do with those murders, and you know it."

Church started to rise. "Did he tell you that? Just let me at him!"

The inspector shoved him back in the chair. "Not much I won't! I'm going to keep you right here till I get the truth out of you. First, I want to know how you made that fellow Parks confess to a crime he never committed."

"But he did do it!" Church cried. "He signed a confession. Let me talk to him again —"

"Sit down," Newmark snapped. "Parks is innocent. We know that now. How did you make him confess?"

"You know he's innocent?" Church queried. "Well then, I might as well tell you. I simply hypnotised him."

"You — *what*?"

"You don't believe me? Bring Parks here and I'll prove it to you."

Parks was brought in. Church stood squarely in front of him and commanded: "Look me in the eye, Leon! That's right. Now then, smile!"

Parks, who had been almost crying only a minute before, began to smile.

"Now, Leon, speak the truth. You had nothing to do with those murders?"

"No, Harvey."

"What were you doing on Thursday?"

"I was working in Gus Benario's garage."

"You're feeling happy now, aren't you, Leon?"

"Yes, Harvey." Parks was smiling and his eyes were shining.

"Laugh, Leon!"

Parks laughed gaily.

Church looked at the officers with a satisfied smile. "You see? That's how it's done. I simply hypnotise him and he says anything I tell him to say."

But the officers were in no mood to admire this display of hypnotic power.

Exasperated, they sent Parks from the room and started afresh on Church.

"Come clean now!" they ordered him. "Quit stalling. Who helped you kill those men?"

"I guess Wilder must have killed them," said Church. "Wilder and some other guy."

But Wilder had an ironclad alibi. The foreman at the shoe factory and a dozen other employees told the detectives that Wilder had put in a full day Thursday at his job, and his time clock stub proved that he had.

When Inspector Newmark gave this information to Church, the suspect laughed and said: "It must have been two other fellows. Anyway, that seems to let Wilder out."

"Yes, it lets Wilder out and it lets you in. We know that you killed those men. Confess!"

But Church wasn't ready to admit anything. They had to pound at him for hours before he finally broke. At last he asked in a hoarse whisper: "Can I see my mother?"

"You can see your mother," Newmark told him, "after you've confessed — not before."

There was a pause. For a long while Church sat in thoughtful silence.

"All right," he whispered at last. "I'll tell you everything. I killed both of them."

"Who helped you?"

"Nobody helped me. I did it alone."

The stenographer was called again to take down another confession. Inspector Newmark had thought the "confession" of Parks was incredible, but it was no more extraordinary than the one that now came from Church.

"We drove to my house in the Packard," he said, "Daugherty, Ausmus, and myself. I told them I had part of the money in the basement and asked Daugherty to come inside with me. We went to the basement together. Ausmus stayed outside in the car.

"When Daugherty entered the basement I twisted his hands behind his back and snapped the handcuffs on them. Then I grabbed the baseball bat and slugged him over the head with it. He toppled over and began lashing out at me with his feet. I grabbed a piece of rope and tied his legs together.

"I heard the door open then, and when I looked around I saw Ausmus standing there. I did the same thing to him that I'd done to Daugherty, except that I had to tie his hands. I slugged him on the head with the baseball bat and knocked him to the floor.

"Both their faces were all bloody now, and I guess

the sight of that blood drove me insane. Anyway, I mauled and slashed them with everything I could lay my hands on, till they were covered with blood. I hit them with the hammer. I hacked them with the hatchet. I seemed to go completely off my nut. I wanted to mash them both into a bleeding pulp.

"I washed the blood off my hands," Church went on, "and went upstairs and got Mother and took her for a ride in the Packard. When we got back home that night I went down to the basement, picked up Daugherty and carried him out to the car. I drove to the Desplaines River and heaved his body into the water.

"Then I went back home for Ausmus. He was still breathing, and I found some cloth in the basement — an old brassière of my mother's — and jammed it down his throat. I picked up his body and carried it out to the garage. I backed my old car out and dug a hole to bury him in.

"I threw him in the hole, face down, and jumped up and down on the back of his neck. Then I covered him with cinders and rolled the car inside so that it covered the spot where I'd buried him.

"And that," said Harvey Church in conclusion, "is how the whole thing happened."

Coroner Hoffman, who had listened to this with incredulity, demanded, "Who helped you do all that?"

"Nobody helped me," said Church with a touch of impatience. "I did it all alone."

The coroner was still sceptical. "Daugherty," he said, "weighed 220 pounds. You weigh 135. How could you overpower him, handcuff him, murder him, and carry him to and from that car unless you had somebody to help you?"

Church said, "Get me a set of handcuffs and a man

who weighs as much as Daugherty, and I'll show you how I did it."

Among the detectives in the room was Sergeant "Billy" McCarthy, who weighed upward of 220 pounds. He volunteered for the demonstration and gave Church a pair of handcuffs.

In a twinkling Church had the sergeant's hands cuffed behind his back. Then he lifted him from the floor and flung him across his shoulder and marched around the room with him. He lowered him to the floor, picked him up and again repeated his trip around the room.

The others stared in astonishment. The performance seemed beyond belief, yet there it was!

Hoffman, however, was still dissatisfied. "If you killed those men alone," he persisted, "why did you drag in Parks and Wilder?"

"You seemed to think some other guys did it," said Church, "so I dug up a pair for you."

"Now tell us," said Captain Mullen, "why you wanted to kill those men."

"I didn't want to kill them," said Church, "till I saw their blood. That seemed to drive me mad, like I told you, and I started to slaughter them."

"Why did you entice Daugherty into your basement and handcuff him?"

"It was the only way I could get the car. I hadn't enough money to pay for it."

"So you killed Daugherty, and then killed Ausmus in order to get an automobile. Is that right?"

"I guess that's right," said Church.

After he had read and signed two copies of his confession he was allowed to see his mother. When he told her what he had done she became hysterical and collapsed.

Church's unmarried sister had arrived from St.

Paul and was also there. She told officers that Harvey had suffered a severe fall when a boy and was often irresponsible ...

Meanwhile thousands of morbidly curious people were milling around Church's home. When he was taken there to re-enact the double murder the police had to rope-off the street to restrain the crowds.

Church was indicted for murder, tried, convicted and sentenced to hang.

The entire case, from start to finish, had been filled with the unbelievable; but now came the most incredible thing of all.

When they locked Harvey Church in the death cell he hypnotised himself!

For days and nights he lay in a stupor, mind and body paralysed, to all appearance dead. He had boasted to guards, when they locked him in, that he would "not be present" at the execution — and apparently he knew what he was talking about.

The warden thought Church was shamming and called in doctors to examine him. The physicians used every test known to medical science — even touching lighted matches to his skin — but nothing could awaken him from his hypnotic sleep.

Coroner Hoffman, still clinging to his theory that more than one person was involved in the double murder, believed that Church had been drugged in jail "to keep him from talking." He asked Church's mother and sister to permit him to perform an autopsy after the execution in order to determine whether Church was really in a comatose condition or the victim of some powerful drug; but they refused consent.

So the coroner issued a public statement: "I still believe that Harvey Church did not commit those two murders unaided. I suspect at least one other man was implicated in the double crime. Church is a weakling, physically and mentally; yet he stands convicted of the weirdest double murder in the criminal history of Chicago, perhaps of the entire United States. His lips have been sealed. He is going to the gallows mentally dead. Why?"

Church was doomed to die on the gallows at 3.54 a.m. on March 4th, 1922 — less than six months after the handcuffed body of Bernard Daugherty was found floating in the Desplaines River.

A few minutes before the death march was scheduled to start, a Salvation Army chaplain entered the prisoner's cell. Church lay on his bunk like a lump of clay. No movement. No sign of life. His eyes were closed and he seemed quite dead.

The chaplain knelt beside the bunk and said close to his ear: "Repeat after me the Lord's Prayer. '*Our Father which art in Heaven ...*'"

There was no response. Church lay apparently lifeless.

Two deputies entered the death cell. "All right, Harvey. Time to go."

There was still no response from the inert body.

The deputies crossed to the bunk and lifted Church to his feet. His eyes did not open. He was like a limp rag. Had the deputies not held him up, he would have slumped to the floor.

This was something new in their experience. The man not only couldn't walk; he couldn't even stand.

So they lifted Church from his bed, sat him in an ordinary kitchen chair and then lifted the chair to their shoulders. He slumped limply and would have fallen out had they not held him in place. His head sagged forward on his chest. His eyes were still closed.

Thus they carried him to the gallows and placed

him on the trap, still slouched unconscious against his bonds in the wooden chair.

The noose was fastened around his neck. This pulled his head up, but his eyes did not open.

Sheriff Charles Peters said to him: "Harvey W. Church, have you anything to say?"

There was no response from the inert form; no sign of life whatever.

Sheriff Peters motioned to a deputy. The deputy slipped a white sack over Church's head. The sheriff gave the signal to spring the trap.

There was a click and the floor fell away from beneath the chair.

The chair dropped from under the man's body, struck the cement floor below, bounded away and came to rest against a concrete post. But the corpse of Harvey Church hung suspended in mid-air at the end of the hangman's rope.

Harvey Church,
arrowed and right.
His statement
staggered Chicago
homicide detectives

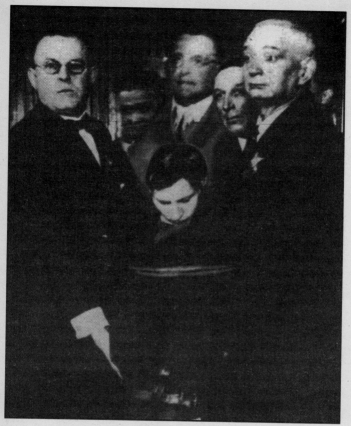

Double-killer is carried to the gallows in a self-hypnotic trance

2
THE GHOST CHILDREN
CHARFIELD, OCTOBER 13TH, 1928

Some mysteries remain forever inexplicable. What happened near the Cotswold village of Charfield on Saturday, October 13th, 1928, is one of them. It concerns two children from nowhere whose lives were suddenly snuffed out. For all that is known of them they might as well have been phantoms. They were described as "ghost-children," and their story was so incredible that it was suggested they never existed. But they did, and their remains were interred in a Charfield churchyard. "Two Unknown" was inscribed on their gravestone, and their fate was to have an equally puzzling sequel: the mysterious suicide of a former chief constable.

Henry Haines knew that the children were not spectres. He knew they were flesh and blood because he saw them, and that made him unique. He was the only person known to have seen them alive.

Haines was a railway porter at Gloucester station, and when the 10 p.m. express from Leeds arrived at 4.56 a.m. on its way to Bristol he boarded the train to collect and punch the passengers' tickets. He hadn't much time because the express was running five minutes late, but he remembered two of the passengers in particular.

One, he said later, was a boy of 11 or 12, the other

a girl of about nine. They were in a compartment at the front of the train, the boy sitting with his back to the engine. A school book lay face-down on the seat beside him. The girl sat facing him, and Haines remembered them because it struck him as odd that two children were travelling so late, unaccompanied by an adult.

In the following days the children were to strike everyone as strange, when their presence on that train in the early hours of the morning became as big a mystery as their identity.

They made headlines, along with 13 other fatally injured fellow-passengers, because at Charfield the express piled into two goods trains. With 41 injured in addition to those killed, the accident shocked the whole nation.

It also became intriguing. All the dead were identified with two exceptions. Nobody could put names to the two small, charred corpses pulled from the wreckage of a compartment near the front of the express.

The train's coaches were gaslit. Gas had leaked and caught fire in the collision, and the blaze had raged for 12 hours. By the time it was extinguished all the injured had been removed and taken to hospital. Only the dead remained for examination by Dr. H. Walsingham Ward, who had been called in by the police from his home nearby at Wootton-under-Edge. One of the corpses had been found on a bridge spanning the cutting where the accident occurred. The passenger had been catapulted there by the impact.

Turning to the last two bodies to be recovered, the doctor found that one was that of a boy of about 11; the other was the corpse of a girl aged around seven. The fire had raged so fiercely that two small shoes were all that was left of their clothing. About nine inches long, the shoes appeared to be a pair and Dr. Ward thought they had probably belonged to the boy.

A verdict of accidental death on all 15 victims was recorded by the coroner at the inquest a week later, but two of the dead were not named. Nobody had come forward to say who they were. It was thought that the parents were perhaps overseas, away on holiday or otherwise out of touch, and that the authorities would hear from them as soon as they learned what had happened to the children. But weeks, months and then years passed without the slightest glimmer of light being thrown on the mystery of the little victims' identity. We know no more about them today than was known in 1928.

Some people found it impossible to believe that two children could suffer such a death and never be claimed. They suggested that it was all some kind of hoax, and that the two children had not been on the train. But Henry Haines, Dr. Ward and the police sergeant who had recovered the bodies knew what they had seen. And there was the further evidence of that gravestone inscription, "Two Unknown," to refute an article which appeared in *The Times* under the heading "Great Myth Exploded."

Further proof that such things could happen came in 1944 with the burial of a child known only as "Little Miss 1565" ... the number being that on her coffin. She was one of 160 people who had perished when fire swept through a circus marquee at Hartford, Connecticut. She was aged about six, with curly brown hair, and her face was virtually untouched by the fire. She was therefore photographed, her picture appearing in newspapers throughout the United States in a bid to identify her. But she remains

"Little Miss 1565" to this day.

In the case of the children buried at Charfield, it was speculated that they were illegitimate, their death coming as a relief to parents who did not wish to be linked with them. Curiosity about their identity was rekindled in 1929, when on the anniversary of their deaths a veiled woman in black entered the Charfield churchyard.

She knelt at the children's grave, and when she left it was seen that she had placed flowers under the engraving "Two Unknown." She spoke to nobody and all that those who saw her could say of her was that she was a stranger. But her visit reinforced the theory that the children had been born out of wedlock to someone important, someone whose reputation had been saved by their demise.

The mysterious woman appeared again a year later, and rumours now began to connect her with the disgraced former Chief Constable of Bristol, James Watson, who had been dismissed for misusing public money by sending some of his staff on private holidays. He had subsequently left the city, but it was said that a man closely resembling him had accompanied the veiled woman to the churchyard on her second visit, waiting for her in a car while she went to the grave of the "Two Unknown."

The next news of him came just before Christmas in 1930 when a Bristol solicitor, James Hapgood, received a cryptic telegram from London: MEET ME WATERLOO BRIDGE TOMORROW NIGHT — J. WATSON.

Hapgood travelled the 120 miles from Bristol's Temple Meads station to Paddington and had a brief meeting with the ex-Chief Constable, but the solicitor never divulged what was said.

Watson's body was found two days later in the

Pleasure Gardens at Eastbourne. An open cut-throat razor lay nearby. Although the coroner recorded an open verdict, the death was assumed to be suicide. The mysterious veiled lady was never seen again, and Hapgood died shortly afterwards, taking the secrets of that London meeting to his grave.

The railway accident in which the unidentified children perished also turned out to have a strong element of mystery, raising questions which were never answered.

Initially it seemed that the accident was simply the outcome of a combination of circumstances. It was misty — but not foggy enough for Signalman Button at Charfield to call for detonators to be placed along the line to warn approaching trains of a signal ahead. Button tested the visibility by looking out along the line at his distant "fog object," an indicator installed for that purpose. If he could see it, detonators weren't needed. It was visible, so none were requested.

A five-minute delay had been caused by a goods train making an unscheduled stop for water at Charfield station. This prompted Button to divert a second goods train proceeding in the same direction into a siding on the opposite side of the main line to avoid delaying the express.

As the goods train was being shunted across the main down line an empty goods train travelling from Westerleigh to Gloucester was approaching Charfield in the opposite direction.

Button had set signals at danger to warn the approaching express, but a glance at his track circuit indicator, an electric device triggered by an oncoming train, told him that those warnings had not been heeded.

In his report on the accident the Board of Trade

inspector was later to say: "All the conditions were hostile. Ten seconds later there would have been no obstruction ... the existence of the bridge, the simultaneous movement of two trains in the opposite direction, the misty atmosphere and the early morning darkness combined to produce almost the worst possible conditions in which a collision at high speed could occur, and rendered deplorable results inevitable."

All three trains piled into each other. And at the inquest on those killed it was decided that the driver of the express, Henry Ernest Aldington, was responsible. He had failed to observe the Charfield danger signals, and he was consequently committed for trial for manslaughter.

Aldington and his fireman Frank Watt didn't seek to excuse themselves by blaming the darkness, the mist or the absence of fog detonators. Both said that as they approached Charfield they saw that the distant signal was showing green for clear. They therefore assumed that the subsequent home signals would be clear also. But they weren't. Aldington and his fireman failed to see them, and the result was the collision.

The express was going so fast, however, that it is unlikely that Aldington would have been able to stop it in time to avoid a collision even if he had seen the home signals.

He escaped unhurt from the crash, and after doing what he could to help the injured he stormed up to Button the signalman. "What's the meaning of this?" he demanded. "Your distant was off."

The signalman told him that was impossible: there was a safety device locking the signal levers into position at danger. But to remove any doubt, Button checked his electric signal repeater. The distant and home signals couldn't be seen from his box, but his repeater would confirm that they were functioning properly.

He carried out the test, and to his consternation it indicated that the distant signal was showing clear!

It was then found that wreckage from the accident had fouled the signal control wire. When the debris was removed, the signal changed to danger.

Aldington was consequently brought to trial, but because of the element of doubt he was acquitted.

If the distant signal was showing clear, as Aldington and his fireman claimed, there could be only two causes. Some other foreign object could have fouled the wire before the accident ... but none was found in the investigation. That left the only other alternative. Had somebody sabotaged the signal by pulling the wire?

That would mean that the railway disaster was no accident, and with that possibility the story came full-circle. For just as the identity of those two children was to remain forever a mystery, so was the enigma of the distant signal never explained.

Nor was another curious circumstance. It was believed that the veiled woman in black must have known who the children were. On the two anniversaries when she visited their grave she was seen by several people. So why did none of them approach her and ask her?

The horrendous rail crash at Charfield. What strange link did it have with the suicide of the former Chief Constable of Bristol, James Watson?

3
AMITYVILLE
LONG ISLAND, NOVEMBER 12TH, 1974

Was it haunted? That's what everyone wondered about the three-storey shingled Dutch colonial house at Amityville, Long Island. True, the present residents had not been troubled by anything unusual ... but their predecessors had moved out after only 28 days. They had been driven out, they said, by the supernatural.

And if ghosts had the right to walk anywhere, it was at this house which until November 1974 was the home of a garage service manager, Ronald DeFeo Sr., and his family. But all that changed on Wednesday, November 13th.

The first intimation of anything wrong came at 6.27 p.m. with a phone call to the police.

"Help! Help me! My family's dead ... murdered!" said a man's voice.

"Who's that speaking?" asked the duty officer.

"My name is Ronald DeFeo junior," said the caller. He sounded shaky and excited.

"What's your address?"

"I'm calling from a tavern down the street ... My home is at 112 Ocean Avenue ... I'll go right home and wait for you there ..."

An alert went out to a police car manned by Patrolman Kenneth Greguski to proceed to that address and investigate the report. The officer reached the scene in less than two minutes.

As he started up the driveway to the front door, he noticed a collection of miniature plaster figurines on the lawn. They consisted of a replica of St. Anthony holding a child in his arms, surrounded by three girls kneeling in prayer.

At the door, Greguski was met by a well-built young man with a beard. "I made the call to the police," he said. "I'm Ronald DeFeo..."

"What happened?"

"My mother ... my father ... my brothers and sisters ... They're all dead ... Somebody killed them ... In their rooms..."

Twenty-three-year-old DeFeo led Greguski into the house and up a red-carpeted circular staircase to the first floor. Just beyond the landing he took the policeman through an open door into the master bedroom. The lights were all shining brightly.

Greguski saw a man and woman lying face-down in a king-sized bed. They were dressed in their night-clothes — the man in blue, flowered pyjamas, the woman in a pink negligee. Both were obviously dead, but what startled the policeman even more than the sight of the two bodies was the position of their hands. They were clasped behind their heads!

The police report would show that the victims in the master bedroom were DeFeo's 43-year-old father, Ronald DeFeo senior, and his wife Louise, 42. After confirming that the couple were dead, Greguski asked their son: "Where are the others?"

"I'll show you," DeFeo replied, leading the officer out of the room and a short distance down the hall to another open door. As the policeman entered this room he saw two more bodies, each lying on one of the twin beds. These victims also had their hands clasped behind their heads. They turned out to be the youngest members of the DeFeo family — nine-year-old John and Mark, aged 11. They too were dead.

"Is that it?" Greguski asked their brother as he eyed the grisly scene.

"No ... there are two more ..."

DeFeo led the policeman into the room next door and showed him his sister Allison, 14, who also lay face-down in her bed — and with her hands clasped behind her head. She was also dead.

"Where's the other one?" the policeman inquired.

DeFeo walked out of the room and went upstairs to the second floor. Greguski followed and was shown into another bedroom. There lay DeFeo's 18-year-old sister Dawn. Like the other victims, she lay dead on her bed and her hands were folded behind her head.

Greguski hurried downstairs to the kitchen and phoned the police station. "Six DOA's," he reported to the duty officer. "They were all murdered."

Although the Amityville police maintain law and order in their community, they are not geared for handling homicide cases. These are investigated by the Suffolk County police.

The call to Homicide brought half a dozen detectives, headed by Lieutenant Thomas A. Richmond. As they went from room to room of the house, they were stunned by the similarity in the positions of the bodies. Their immediate reaction was that this could be a gangland murder, or some sort of macabre ritual-type killing. None of the detectives had seen anything remotely like it.

While Richmond took Greguski aside and asked him for a rundown on the circumstances under which he found the bodies, young DeFeo sat in the living-room giving background information on his family and himself to other detectives. As he spoke to the investigators, a large white sheepdog sat quietly at one end of the room.

"It's a damn shame he can't talk," DeFeo said. "If he could, I'll bet he could tell us who murdered my family."

The dog had apparently been in the house when Greguski arrived, but the policeman didn't see him until after making his tour of the four bedrooms and phoning in his report on the multiple slayings. The dog, named Shaggy, had apparently been hiding in one of the other rooms.

Greguski told Richmond how he was met at the door by Ronald DeFeo and taken upstairs to each of the bedrooms to view the bodies.

"You say the kid came home, found the bodies, then went to a ginmill to call the police?" Richmond asked.

"That's what my duty officer told me — and that's what DeFeo said," Greguski replied.

"What the hell was wrong with using one of the house phones?" Richmond demanded. "Where's this ginmill?"

"It's about a block and a half away ... down on Merrick Avenue. It's called Henry's."

Richmond turned to two of his men. "Take a run down there and check out the story," he directed. "And while you're on your way, count the number of houses between here and the tavern. I want to know how many other phones young Ronnie passed up in the biggest crisis of his life."

Meanwhile, Dr. Howard Adelman, the medical examiner, was studying each of the bodies before removing them to the morgue for post-mortems. His findings indicated that Mr. and Mrs. DeFeo had each been shot twice in the back, while John and Mark were each shot once in the back. Allison and Dawn were killed by single bullets to the back of the head. It appeared that they were all asleep when they were killed. Following the post-mortems, which more or less bore out his findings at the scene, Dr. Adelman set the time of deaths at between 10 p.m. and midnight on Tuesday, November 12th.

Meanwhile, Richmond was eliciting a few more facts from the only surviving member of the murdered family. DeFeo said he'd woken at about 7 a.m. on Wednesday morning and had gone to work at Brigante-Karl Buick, the Brooklyn garage where his father was service manager and young Ronald was a mechanic. The car dealership was owned by the senior DeFeo's father-in-law, Richmond learned.

The lieutenant asked DeFeo about his activities for the last 24 hours. DeFeo started with Tuesday, when he said he went to work with his father. It was usual for them to leave in the morning and drive together to the garage. They would also return home together. That was the way it was on Tuesday, young DeFeo told the detective. But after driving back home with his father on Tuesday evening, DeFeo explained, he went out again and didn't return until very late. He went straight to bed, and the next morning drove to work without his father ...

The story didn't satisfy Richmond, but he didn't press for better answers. He wanted some other questions answered first before broadening the investigation.

He assigned two detectives to drive the 37 miles to Coney Island, Brooklyn, to interview workers at Brigante-Karl Buick for information on the elder DeFeo and his son. Richmond also wanted neighbours to be questioned about the family's character and habits.

The investigation was not many hours old before the detectives learned that the slain Ronald DeFeo Sr. was the nephew of Peter DeFeo, a 72-year-old reputed capo in the Vito Genovese crime family. Peter DeFeo's most recent run-in with the authorities had occurred in 1968, when he was arrested and charged with trying to obtain kickbacks from the Teamsters Union pension fund. On another occasion, Peter DeFeo had been charged with murder, but acquitted.

There was only the slightest suspicion that the deaths of Ronald DeFeo, his wife, two sons and two daughters were the work of the underworld. Children and wives are not usually marked for death in gangland contracts — and the target of a mob killing is not usually murdered in his home. In general practice, the mob informs a member that he has been marked for death, tells him the reason, and then kills him away from home.

Nevertheless, police were not overlooking any possibility.

Ronald DeFeo Sr's past, however, was as clean as a whistle. For despite his relationship to Peter DeFeo, the nephew's closest friends had been prominent policemen.

Moreover, the slain DeFeo and his father-in-law Brigante were active in many of the affairs of patrolmen's associations. DeFeo frequently attended their convention, while Brigante often bought tables for his family at their dinner-dances. Many policemen bought cars and had them serviced at Brigante-Karl Buick.

In contrast, young Ronald DeFeo had already had several brushes with the law. When the rundown at police headquarters was made on the lone survivor of the massacre, it was found that he had a record of arrests that included larceny and narcotics.

More recently — in October, a month before the murders — Ronald had been given $23,000 of his firm's money to deposit in a bank. But he returned to the Buick agency's showroom to report that he'd been held up in the street and robbed of the cash and cheques.

His father hadn't believed him and harassed his son relentlessly to return the deposit. But Ronald insisted that he didn't have it and stuck to his story of the robbery. In the midst of the tension caused by the almost nightly arguments between father and son at home, the elder DeFeo bought Ronald's sister Dawn a car. The investigation showed that Ronald was further incensed over that, since he had been after his father to get him a car of his own.

Despite this significant background on Ronald DeFeo, Richmond and his detectives could not tie the son to the killings. But he was by this time the prime suspect because of several key discoveries made in the early hours of the investigation.

One of these concerned a .35-calibre Marlin rifle, part of the family collection, which was now missing. The other weapons — a .22-calibre rifle, a double-barrelled shotgun and a pellet gun — were in their racks. But the Marlin was not, and young DeFeo could not explain what had happened to it.

Since no death weapon had been found in the house or in the search of the grounds, Richmond and his detectives suspected that the Marlin was used in the killings. Their suspicions would later be confirmed by ballistics experts, who recovered the bullets from the mattresses and identified them as .35-calibre rifle slugs.

By then Ronald DeFeo had undergone four hours of continuous questioning at his house. And when detectives found themselves getting few answers to their satisfaction, it was decided to bring the young man to the homicide squad's offices in Hauppague for further investigation.

Meanwhile, the detectives Richmond had sent to Henry's Tavern returned. They had counted 24 houses between the DeFeo residence and the ginmill, any one of which Ronald could have stopped at to phone the police. They also uncovered a goldmine of information that supported Richmond's early suspicions of the son.

In questioning a number of patrons at Henry's, detectives found out that DeFeo had been at the bar the previous Monday evening and had made inquiries among some of his drinking companions about where he could obtain a silencer for a gun. That information seemed to provide an answer to the question that Richmond and the other detectives had been asking from the beginning of their investigation — how was it possible to shoot six people, one at a time, in a single household and not rouse one of them from their sleep?

"It is the most incredible thing, when you think about it," Dr. Adelman said. "The noise of a rifle like the Marlin certainly should have awakened some of the others in the house."

Obviously, it hadn't. So from the start, detectives speculated on three possible theories of how the six were murdered: (1) the killer had a silencer on the rifle; (2) there was more than one killer; or (3) the family was drugged.

Detectives from the Suffolk County police scientific investigation unit found the remains of a beef stew in the refrigerator. Young DeFeo confirmed that this was the meal his mother had served the family for Tuesday's dinner. The stew was taken to the police laboratory for analysis.

The tests and the subsequent toxicological studies of the contents of the victims' stomachs showed no traces of any drug that might have been employed as a tranquilliser. So that left the first two possibilities — that the family had been shot by a killer who used a silencer on the rifle, or that he had an accomplice who held the other victims pinned in their rooms while the slayer went about executing the DeFeos one by one.

At 6.27 p.m. on November 14th — exactly 24 hours to the minute after his initial call to police — Ronald DeFeo was formally booked on six charges of murder.

At his arraignment the next morning, he was remanded to the Suffolk County jail in Riverhead. The court also ordered a psychiatric examination. Meanwhile, on November 18th, a Suffolk County grand jury returned a murder indictment against him. Some weeks later, the psychiatrists found Ronald DeFeo competent to stand trial.

This was held before Justice Thomas N. Stark in the latter part of 1975 in Riverhead, the Suffolk County seat. Assistant District Attorney Gerard Sullivan, a tough, hard-nosed prosecutor, quickly set the stage for combat with the defence by putting a former friend of DeFeo, Frank Davidge, on the witness-stand.

Davidge stated that he'd been a close friend at one time and told how he and DeFeo double-dated on one occasion in the summer of 1972. When the evening was coming to a close, DeFeo got out of the car to escort his date to her door. But before he reached there, he rushed back to the car, pulled a rifle from under the front seat and pointed it at his date's head.

Davidge testified that he jumped out of the car and

intervened. When he asked DeFeo why he had acted so strangely, his friend could give no reason.

Again in that year DeFeo and his friend went hunting. In the woods, Davidge said, he caught a glimpse of DeFeo aiming at him. "I dodged behind a tree just in time to avoid being hit by three shots," the witness testified. Again, there was no explanation.

In the spring of 1973, Davidge said, his friend grabbed a shotgun off the wall of his bedroom and without provocation fired at Davidge's head twice. The gun misfired — and Davidge, lucky to be alive, said this ended his friendship with DeFeo.

When Ronald DeFeo took the witness-stand he at first protested his innocence. He said he didn't believe he was guilty when he signed statements and made oral confessions to detectives after the bodies were discovered.

He was then shown photos of his murdered mother and brother Mark. "Do you know who these people are?" defence counsel William Weber asked.

"I never saw them before in my life," DeFeo replied.

"Did you kill your mother? Did you kill Mark?"

"I'm not guilty as charged," DeFeo answered.

Shown a photo of his father on his deathbed, DeFeo again denied knowing who it was. But then Weber asked: "Did you kill your father?"

"I killed him in self-defence," DeFeo replied.

"Did you have any help?" Justice Stark interposed.

"No," DeFeo answered. "I did it alone."

Earlier testimony had depicted the accused as a violent character who couldn't get along with anyone in school or in a job. And DeFeo himself now sketched a picture of constant hostility, bickering and physical abuse in the home.

When DeFeo was 12, he said, he was expelled

from school in Brooklyn and went home to tell his parents. His father became very angry and told him: "You're not my son. I had to marry your mother when she was six months gone. She's a whore!"

According to DeFeo, his parents then got into a fight. When he tried to break it up, they turned on him. "She tried to kill my father," DeFeo said. "He threw a chair at her and it hit me. It knocked out my front teeth. They had to be capped. He was always fighting with everyone in the house."

From the witness-stand, DeFeo painted a self-portrait of interminable aggression against authority. In his view the teachers in his schools were always in the wrong. He admitted that he once beat a nun. "Teachers provoked me," he testified. "They were wrong. I was always right."

That same attitude prevailed in later years when he went out to earn a living. He never held a job for more than a few months. He also became a drug addict, though he kicked the habit with the help of a doctor because it was affecting his health. A year later, in 1971, he began getting his kicks from alcohol. He also began carrying a handgun. He got into several violent scrapes while under the influence of drink. He then went back to drugs and took heroin. Why?

"The situation in the house was getting worse. I could just about take it with drugs," DeFeo told the court.

One of the hairiest encounters occurred a year before the family was murdered, according to the defendant ... "I heard my parents fighting in their bedroom. My mother was screaming for help. My sister Dawn came running into my room to get me to break it up. I refused.

"But Dawn wouldn't stop pleading. 'Daddy's

killing Mommy!' she cried. 'You've got to help!'

"I then took a 12-gauge shotgun off the wall in my room and went into my parents' bedrooms. I found my mother lying on the floor, my father standing over her.

"'Listen, you fat bastard!' I said. 'Get off that woman now, or I'll kill you.' He froze. I pulled the trigger once, click — twice, click again. It didn't go off."

The father then proclaimed that God had wrought a miracle, that the Lord was "behind me." He made the entire family hang religious pictures throughout the house — and had statues placed outside on the front and back lawns.

A year later, however, Divine Providence had failed to intervene when young Ronald set about wiping out the family of six.

In his closing argument, Defence Attorney Weber asked the jury: "What more proof of a diseased mind can there be than Ronald DeFeo Jr. being charged with killing his own family? Anybody to do this, *has* to have a diseased mind, *has* to be sick."

He said that DeFeo, by admitting the killings on the witness-stand, "has given up the possibility of freedom for the certainty of everlasting confinement — whether it is in a mental institution or jail."

Prosecutor Sullivan countered: "There's no question that something is wrong with Ronnie. Normal people don't kill other people ... They certainly don't kill *six* people. The cold, calm, deliberate way in which the murders were carried out proves that DeFeo wasn't acting in the heat of passion, or acting under extreme emotional disturbance ... He selected a time to kill all the members of his family as they slept in their beds, under the darkness of night.

"There sits an abnormal person all right! But his

disorder is in having an anti-social personality, not a psychosis!"

Sullivan told the jury that DeFeo retrieved the shell casings after he'd triggered the bullets into his family — "he had to dip into a pool of his sister's blood to get one of them. He took the casings, as well as clothing he had been wearing, some of it blood-stained, and disposed of everything in the bay off Amityville and in a Brooklyn sewer drain ... This was a planned, systematic act to separate himself from the crime, an indication that he knew what he had done was wrong."

After two days of deliberation, the jury returned a guilty verdict on each of the six murder counts.

On December 4th, 1975, Justice Stark imposed six consecutive prison terms of 25 years to life — a minimum imprisonment of 150 years. In doing so, he called the massacre "the most heinous and abhorrent known to Long Island ... I am ordering the maximum jail term, because I am of the belief that he represents a clear danger to others — that is, that he may well kill again."

Yet after Ronald DeFeo was removed from society, the story of the family massacre took on new and incredible dimensions.

The DeFeos' former home in Amityville was bought by George Lutz, a surveyor, who settled in with his wife and children. But not for long. Moving out less than a month later, they claimed that "strange forces" were causing them to depart for California.

Jay Anson's *The Amityville Horror*, a book devoted to the Lutzes' experiences in the house where six had been slain, told of green slime oozing through the keyholes, the mysterious creaking of floorboards, and bodies levitating six feet from the floor.

The account was debunked by psychic research groups, Amityville Village Historical Society, the DeFeos' former neighbours and the subsequent occupants of the house. But five million copies of Anson's book were sold and it became the basis of a popular film. Both appealed to those who preferred to believe that, dead though they were, the DeFeos wouldn't lie down.

The book was exposed as sheer fantasy. As a witness it cited a policeman who didn't exist. It described psychic researchers investigating the "phenomena," whereas none had actually gone near the place. But that didn't stop self-styled witches, Satanworshippers and other assorted weirdos from descending on the house.

Ironically, the wildest imaginings of *The Amityville Horror* were eclipsed by grim reality. The policeman called to the house could testify to that. What they saw was horror enough for anyone.

Ronald DeFeo. *The Amityville Horror* by Jay Anson became a best seller

Death house. This was the scene at Amityville on Long Island when six members of the DeFeo family were found murdered

4

SEANCE ON THE CRUMBLES
EASTBOURNE, AUGUST 19TH, 1920

If investigation of the murder of Irene Munro had
been left to strictly conventional methods, her killers
might have got away with it. But they didn't. They
were snared by a detective from Scotland Yard ...
with help from a spiritualist. The scene was the
Crumbles, a then desolate stretch of shingle beach
near the Sussex resort of Eastbourne. The time was
midnight, chosen to avoid sightseers. A seance was
about to take place. A seance held to trap Irene's
slayers ...

Irene Munro lived in London, where her mother
was a housekeeper in Queen's Gate, South Kensington. Summer had come and with it Mrs. Munro's
wish to see her family again in Scotland. But Irene, a
17-year-old typist, had other ideas. Mrs. Munro
didn't object. It was to be expected. Teenager though
she was, Irene was becoming a young woman. Mrs.
Munro could understand her not wanting to spend
her holiday making polite small talk with elderly
relatives in Portobello.

So when Irene said she'd rather go to the South
Coast, her mother helped with her holiday plans: how
much money she'd need, what to pack, how to book
suitable accommodation. Soon everything was arranged. Irene was to spend her fortnight's break at

393 Seaside, Eastbourne. And when she arrived on the bright Monday morning of August 16th, 1920, her holiday landlady Mrs. Ada Wynniatt was waiting to greet her.

So was somebody else she'd meet later. Two somebodies, to be precise. A couple of men for whom life was one long holiday, thanks to girls like Irene.

Mrs. Wynniatt warmed to her new guest. Irene was no brash Londoner. There was still a touch of Scot about her and she seemed so young, still with her schoolgirl looks. She was pleasant, well spoken and seemed sensible, but the motherly Mrs. Wynniatt couldn't help wondering if she wasn't perhaps a little naive.

That's what Jack and Bill wondered too. They were the spiders, she the fly. A fly with a handbag which they guessed held her holiday money. Only a few pounds saved up from her wages, but a few pounds went a long way in 1920.

They seemed an ill-matched pair, Jack and Bill. Jack was the younger, had been in the navy and had the bright and breezy air of a sailor. At 19 he wasn't much older than Irene. Bill was 29 but didn't admit to it, just as he didn't let on that he was married. Despite their age gap, Jack and Bill had two things in common. Both were unemployed. Both intended to stay that way, doing as little as possible, enjoying life at the expense of the likes of Irene.

They spotted the Scots girl shortly after she arrived and it wasn't long before they were chatting her up. Someone with a little more experience would have seen through them, would at least have wondered what they did for a living, how they managed to have so much spare time. But not Irene. They weren't bad company. In fact, she was quite attracted by young

Jack. For her, the two men were instant friends in a town of strangers. She was enjoying herself, and that was what holidays were for.

She walked around town and along the promenade with them, her handbag tucked firmly under her arm. When she had a drink with them the bag was not put down. It was never allowed out of her sight, and the care she took of it confirmed her companions' guess at its contents. The young holidaymaker didn't have much, but compared with the two at her side she was loaded, and they were both determined to relieve her of her burden.

It was on Thursday that the trio agreed to meet near the bus stop at the Archery Tavern, on the road leading to Pevensey. Irene was delighted at the chance of having an afternoon ramble across that lonely stretch of pebble beach known as the Crumbles.

She went back to her digs for her midday meal, and was ready to leave again shortly before 3 p.m. When she appeared downstairs Mrs. Wynniatt came into the narrow hall.

"Lovely afternoon," said the landlady. "Going far?"

"Hampden Park. I shan't need an umbrella, shall I?"

"Heavens, no!" Mrs. Wynniatt exclaimed. "The papers say this warm spell is going to last. Weather's always fine as long as the wind isn't bringing any cloud from over Beachy Head."

She opened the front door and Irene went out into the street and hurried away, Mrs. Wynniatt watching her green coat bright in the sunshine as she made her way along Seaside.

It was not far to the Archery Tavern. Irene arrived first, and was waiting at the bus stop when the two men dropped from the platform of a slowing bus. If she noticed that their breath smelled of beer she passed no comment.

Jack was smoking one of the Turkish cigarettes he preferred. She was not aware of it, but Jack, like his older companion, had run through his week's dole money. For men close to destitution they indulged odd tastes and had extravagant spending habits. But then she didn't realise how much encouragement they received from the sight of her handbag tucked under her arm.

The three fell into step, and Jack, who had brought along a walking-stick, kept banging his leg with it, as if it seemed unfamiliar to him.

The two men fell quickly silent after meeting her. They started for the Crumbles, not Hampden Park, and the pace slowed as they trudged across the solid bank of sun-warmed shingle. They walked long beyond the limit of the summer trippers, out across the loneliest stretch of the long beach that wound away towards Pevensey.

"I'm getting tired," said Irene at last.

She stopped, felt in her handbag for her little square of handkerchief, and dabbed at her warm young face.

The two men looked at each other. Bill nodded.

Jack lifted the stick with the metal ferrule, held it ready and then Bill snatched at her handbag. Suddenly startled, the girl clung to it.

"Hey, what do you think ——!"

The metal ferrule caught her in the mouth, forced her teeth apart and drove against the inside of her cheek. She screamed with pain and fell, letting go of her handbag.

"Shut up!" snapped the older man, who held the bag.

But Irene screamed again, panicking at the thought of her money disappearing.

The older man looked around. The younger wet his nervous lips.

"For God's sake do something," he urged.

Bill ran to a piece of discarded concrete. He brought it back. The younger man seemed paralysed as he stood watching while the heavy concrete slab descended with a sickening crunch on Irene's head.

Blood streamed over the shingle. Jack stared at it as though mesmerised. He was shaken awake by the man who had stuffed the handbag into his pocket when he ran for the concrete slab.

"Here, help me bury her! Quick, while no one's about! Hurry, damn it!"

But it was a poor job of burying they did, sweating and cursing and constantly glancing around for fear that they might be interrupted by the arrival of other holidaymakers.

They covered the body in the green coat with shingle well above the reach of the sea at high tide. But they skimped the task, leaving the toe of one shoe peeking through the stones of the shingle beach.

At six o'clock they entered their favourite haunt, the Albemarle, for a drink.

It was Thursday and customers were not spending rashly. The exceptions were Jack and Bill. They not only insisted on the barmaid having a drink with them, but they also ordered drinks for some women lower down the bar.

The little Scots typist's money for her holiday, saved and put away shilling by shilling, was going fast. The Oxford Street firm of accountants that employed her had paid her less than £2 10s. a week.

The next day a small boy wandered off across the Crumbles, searching among rocks and across the pebbly beach for any treasure trove the sea might have cast up in his path. He wandered farther than usual, and was about to turn back when he saw the toe of a shoe sticking up through the grey and white stones. A shoe on a beach was not just a discarded article of footwear to him. It was booty. He began clambering across the shingle to reach his prize and when he stooped down and cleared away the smooth stones he found that he had uncovered not only a shoe, but also a stockinged foot.

He ran away, shouting.

Less than 24 hours after her death, Irene Munro had been discovered.

The police surgeon who was summoned soon saw how Irene had died, but he was puzzled by the laceration he found inside her mouth.

The body was dressed in a thin green summer coat. All the girl's clothes were there, but where was her handbag? The motive for the crime was obvious to the police.

Meanwhile, Mrs. Wynniatt was undergoing her own ordeal. She and her husband had sat up till midnight awaiting the return of Irene.

"Maybe she's staying with some friends," Mr. Wynniatt had suggested, "though she should have let you know."

"I'm really worried about her," his wife told him.

"She'll turn up for breakfast most likely."

But the husband was really only talking to cheer up his wife. He liked the continued absence of the young girl much less than he was prepared to admit. The next morning a letter arrived for Irene. It was postmarked Portobello. Mrs. Wynniatt put it on the living-room mantelpiece to await Irene's return.

It was in the afternoon that the landlady had misgivings about the girl ever reading the letter from her mother in Scotland. A neighbour told her of the discovery of a young girl's body out on the Crumbles. No one seemed to know who she was or where she had come from. The police had been unable to identify her.

Mrs. Wynniatt waited until her husband returned from work.

"You've heard the news?" she said.

"About the body — yes, and I heard there was a green coat. We'll have to go to the police."

Not long after Mr. Wynniatt's return from work, he and his wife stood in a cool room at the local mortuary and looked down at the battered remains of the young girl who had come to stay with them. The surgeon had cleansed the remains of the crushed head, but Mrs. Wynniatt flinched as she saw what the concrete slab had done to the childish features under the cluster of dark curls. She couldn't recognise the remains of the face.

But she said: "That's her coat. I recognise the fur trimming on it."

Chief Inspector Mercer arrived from Scotland Yard and was taken out to the Crumbles. No longer a lonely place, it was now crawling with a crowd of holiday sightseers, who seemed to be turning over every pebble on the beach.

"It'll probably be like this for a week," said a local CID man grimly. "Until they realise that their holiday's slipping away."

Mercer called on Mrs. Wynniatt and learned that in the three days she had been staying at 393 Seaside the girl had received two letters, one with a South Kensington postmark. Mrs. Wynniatt told him that the girl had been concerned about buying a holiday present for someone.

A message was sent to the police in Portobello.

Mrs. Munro's stay in Scotland was abruptly ended. She caught the first train south.

It was not difficult to compute how much the young typist who had worked for a firm of London accountants had had in her handbag when she was murdered. She had not spent much since her arrival in Eastbourne, and her mother knew to within a few shillings how much she had saved up for the holiday.

She had paid Mrs. Wynniatt a pound deposit against the cost of her first week's board and lodging. The weekly cost of the room was 30 shillings. The landlady had seen the pound notes in the handbag when the girl paid her.

Inquiries were begun down that long street called Seaside. Several people recalled seeing the smiling girl in the light green coat with fur trimming. Some had seen her talking to a couple of men, one of them noticeably older than the other, who was nearer the girl's age.

Detectives learned that one of the men had worn a suit with a herring-bone pattern. It had appeared to be new. Many young men wearing similar suits in Eastbourne were stopped and questioned.

The dragnet pulled in a good number for questioning. Most of them had no difficulty in answering satisfactorily the various questions put to them, and they were released. A couple who fell into this category were two friends named Jack Alfred Field and William Thomas Gray.

Field was 19, single, and unemployed. Gray was 29, married, and unemployed. They told the police that on the Thursday morning, the day about which the police were making inquiries, they had both gone to the unemployment bureau to draw their allowances.

There seemed no real reason for detaining them,

although the elder wore a light herring-bone suit. To the police it seemed unlikely that a young girl such as Irene Munro would be associating with a married man.

It was possible that the two men would not have left the police station so easily had they given the investigating officer one additional piece of information — that on the day Irene Munro's body was found both men appeared at a recruiting station and tried to join the army.

Their names and addresses had been noted. To their dismay they heard that it was not possible to enlist immediately.

Meanwhile another investigator was on their trail, a man not restricted to the traditional methods employed by the police. He was Harold Speer, a newspaper reporter, and he had enlisted the services of a spiritualist, Miss Groebel.

"Do you believe that my clairvoyant powers will be of use to you?" she had asked.

"Yes, I do," he had assured her.

She told him that she needed to place herself as near as possible to the spot where Irene Munro had drawn her last breath. She also said she would need to hold items which had belonged to Irene. The reporter had established a good relationship with Chief Inspector Mercer. He told the detective of the seance he proposed. This was not something in which Mercer could become involved in his official capacity, but he lent Speer some of Irene Munro's possessions, which included a blotter that she had used frequently.

As midnight approached, Speer made his way with Miss Groebel to the Crumbles. As they neared the crime-scene, the reporter was later to recall, Miss Groebel "seemed to be groping her way through a mist or fog. With her hands thrust forward, her slender fingers nervously extended, she wandered in ever-narrowing circles ... presently she made some queer, half-articulate sounds and appeared to be in conversation. Then she took her stand definitely — she had found the precise spot where the body was discovered.

"She sat down on the shingle and quickly appeared to be in a trance. Her face was deathly white and her arms hung limply at her sides. Raising her hands, I placed in them the articles I had obtained. She convulsively grasped them and her hands fondled them. Then through the darkness came a voice quite different to Miss Groebel's.

" 'Oh! Pray for me, pray for me! Tell my mother I am sorry!' "

Speer went on to record that the voice declared itself to be that of Irene, saying she had been killed by a man with a large stone. Asked where this was, Miss Groebel promptly pointed to the spot where the concrete slab had been found. The spiritualist could have learned that from the newspapers, but the voice which came from Miss Groebel went on to say something that was new to the investigation: "I see my murderer in a small hotel. It has a white front, and the name is Albemarle."

The reporter passed the information to Mercer. The hotel was already on the detective's list of premises where routine inquiries were to be made. Now it had an especial interest. Police went there and learned that the hotel's saloon bar had recently been frequented by two men often seen in each other's company. They were known as Bill and Jack and for two weeks they had been at the Albemarle in the afternoons and evenings, drinking, smoking and talking ... two men apparently with little else to do.

Yet they were not holidaymakers. They were locals, but had not been seen in the Albemarle's saloon bar since the evening of August 19th — the evening when Irene Munro had met her savage death.

The detectives became even more interested in Bill and Jack when they heard that on that evening both had been flush with money.

"Fairly throwing it about," was how one barmaid described the spending spree. "Bit different from how they were earlier."

"What do you mean?" she was asked.

"Well, about midday they were broke."

The plain-clothes men reported back to Chief Inspector Mercer. He went along to the Albemarle and learned that at midday the two men had entered the pub. They had remained smoking and drinking in the saloon bar until one. Bill had complained of the heat. He was in a herring-bone suit, and had pushed his felt hat well back on his head. Jack had on a dark suit and wore a cloth cap at an angle and pulled well down across his forehead, so that it shielded his eyes. He was smoking what the barmaid called "stinkers" — presumably cigarettes with aromatic tobacco, possibly Turkish.

"Any chance of getting a few drinks on the slate, darling?" one of the pair had asked the barmaid. "You know how it gets on a Thursday."

"I know," the barmaid nodded. "So does the gov'nor. That's why there's no credit."

For an hour after one o'clock the pair were absent from the bar. But they were back by two o'clock. They had a single glass of beer apiece and stayed drinking it until closing time, which was half-past two.

When the tapman came round calling, "Time,

gentlemen!'' they finished their beer and turned towards the door.

"We'll be back about six," one of them called to a barmaid.

Mercer had his dragnet drawn tighter around the Albemarle area. His detectives began making fresh inquiries.

They established that Jack and Bill had been seen walking down the road for some distance after leaving the Albemarle at closing time. They had crossed to a bus stop and had waited for a bus travelling in the direction of the Archery Tavern, where a crucial witness had seen a girl meet the two men as they alighted from the bus.

This witness, a bus conductor, told Mercer that he had caught a bus that day to the Archery where he was to start his route. On the bus were Field and Gray, whom he knew. He said he particularly remembered them because when he got off at the Archery, Field had said, "Too proud to speak now you have a uniform on?" The three of them spoke briefly, then he said: "They were standing at the corner of the Archery Tavern. After I'd had a word or two with them, I walked up and had a little talk with the driver of the bus, and then I was going to proceed to the depot. When I got about a hundred feet away, I happened to look round and I saw a girl come across the road from the shelter where the bus stops, where it turns around. As she was coming across the road she said, 'Hullo, Jack!' When I say she was coming across the road, I mean coming across to where the two men were standing."

This was crucial evidence that linked the two men with Irene that day.

A minute's walk along Seaside, two decorators were working on the outside of 393, where Irene was staying. They saw her leave the house without a coat, walk in the direction of the Archery, then return a few minutes later. Irene then left again wearing her green coat, and soon after the trio passed 393. "They were all talking and Irene was laughing," one of the decorators told Mercer. A date with death had obviously been arranged.

The trio walking in the direction of the Crumbles were also observed by another witness, who was later to give evidence at the Sussex Assizes in Lewes. His name was Wells, and he was a stoker in the Navy. He said he passed close enough to the two men and a girl walking three abreast to notice the walking-stick carried by the younger man. It had a metal ferrule at one end, and the handle was shaped like a dog's head.

The dragnet continued to the edge of the waste shingle that was the Crumbles.

There the police questioned workmen who were brewing their tea in a hut. A couple of them recalled the girl in the green coat on the important Thursday. While they could say little about her companions, they remembered the girl — and that all three had gone on towards the beach.

The police had reason enough to pick up Bill Gray and his younger male companion, whose name they soon discovered was Jack Alfred Field.

It was not long before the pair were arrested. They were seen by Chief Inspector Mercer, who found their stories thin to the point of transparency.

"I'm charging you both with the murder of Irene Munro," he told them.

When their trial opened on December 13th, 1920, the prosecution had a watertight case. It also had a secret, for it was not generally known that Dr. Bernard Spilsbury, the eminent pathologist, had come down from London and examined the remains of the Scots typist.

His notes included the following observation: "Injuries to the left face, consistent with a single blow by the bloodstained stone if the head was resting on the shingle on the right side, accounting for right injuries. From amount of blood extravasated, slow rate of breathing and shock."

The report concluded: "Probably survived for short time — might have been half an hour, but would be deeply unconscious all the time. Death might have been accelerated by weight of shingle on body compressing chest. Thus death may have been due to combined effects of shock and loss of blood and asphyxia. May have been blood on assailant."

The last sentence had been noted by Mercer in conjunction with something told to him by the sharp-eyed barmaid at the Albemarle. When the pair returned to the hotel on that Thursday evening Bill had not been wearing his herring-bone suit. He had changed it for a darker and rather shabby one. He explained this to the barmaid, Dorothy Duckers, by saying that his friend had pushed him into the water.

Neither Field nor Gray looked very interested in the court proceedings, but Field, who was defended by Mr. J. D. Cassels, later to become Mr. Justice Cassels, elected to go into the witness-box and give himself an alibi.

He denied seeing Irene Munro on the day she was murdered, and explained how in the morning he had drawn 29 shillings from the labour exchange and had bought some Turkish cigarettes. This much tallied with his previous statement to the police. He went on to tell how he had met Gray and gone with him to the Albemarle, and how they had returned after lunch and drank beer before leaving at closing time, two-thirty. They had then walked some way along Seaside, caught a bus, and alighted near the Archery Tavern. There was a circus on some waste land nearby, and after going to it they had walked as far as Pevensey Bay. He said they met no girl at the Archery Tavern and they had not gone to the Crumbles.

It was a bold attempt to explain away the fact that they had been seen by a number of persons who had remembered them — but who could also have been mistaken as to precisely where and when.

But both men had been seen with Irene, and the Crown's witnesses were positive as to the where and to the when.

Field and Gray had thought that they could bury their victim long enough to give them a few weeks or even months to make sure of escaping. What they had overlooked in their hurry was the shoe poking through the shingle and pointing at the Sussex sky.

Sir Edward Marshall Hall, who defended Gray, did not advise his client to enter the witness-box and stand up to a cross-examination which might destroy Field's story.

So the defence was left necessarily lop-sided, and the jury drew their own conclusions from the facts.

After summing up by Mr. Justice Avory, the jury retired to consider their verdict. They returned to pronounce both defendants guilty.

Both prisoners appeared before the Court of Appeal, and at this hearing each tried to blame the other for the murder. Gray had already tried to induce a fellow-prisoner at Lewes to give him a bogus alibi.

The appeal was dismissed, and both men were hanged at Wandsworth on February 4th, 1921.

Their trial had been notable for two curious circumstances. The jury, for some reason best known to themselves, recommended mercy because the crime had not been premeditated.

No?

The killers had promised to return that same evening to the Albemarle, and one had invited a barmaid to the cinema at a time when the pockets of both were almost empty.

The second curious circumstance was Jack Field's tendency to fall asleep while counsel for the prosecution was haranguing the jury. This was such a gross contempt of court that Mr. Justice Avory stopped the proceedings when he observed the slumbering prisoner, and directed the attention of an officer of the court to the sleeper in the dock.

Jack Field had to be prodded awake to hear the jury being told why his life was forfeit. He was so uninterested that he had great difficulty in remaining awake.

After all, whatever he was dreaming must have been better than grim reality.

Now, more than 70 years later, Irene and her slayers would never recognise the transformed Crumbles of today. The once empty stretch of shingle has become the site of a complex including waterside homes and a marina. There is also a floating restaurant, its diners unaware that it was nearby that the Crumbles witnessed not only a murder but also a seance: a paranormal session that helped to bring two killers to justice.

Seventeen-year-old Irene Munro. Below, the spot on the Crumbles where her body was found, and the scene of the dramatic seance

Irene Munro's murderers William Gray (left) and Jack Field at their trial

5
HOMICIDE AT BEDTIME
ANSON, TEXAS, SUNDAY, APRIL 2ND, 1939

The first time Mrs. J. L. Feagan had her nightmare she said nothing about it. She tried to put it out of her mind. Then she had the same dream the following night: her elderly mother, Mrs. Viola King, had died suddenly in horrific circumstances.

Mrs. Feagan mentioned the nightmare to her 19-year-old daughter, Dollie, who did her best to reassure her that it was only a dream, and all was well. But when that same chilling vision disturbed Mrs. Feagan's sleep for the third time, she could bear it no longer.

"Call me silly if you wish," she told her daughter at breakfast, "but there's only one thing that'll bring me peace of mind. As soon as you can put a few things in a bag we're driving over to see Grandma."

It was 9.30 in the morning of April 2nd, 1939, when they left their home in San Angelo, Texas, and a little after 4 o'clock when they finally reached the outskirts of Anson, where Mrs. King lived.

The sight of the small town where she had spent a happy childhood with her favourite brothers, Sam and Jack, momentarily drove the look of haunted fear from Mrs. Feagan's face and she cheerfully pointed out — for the hundredth time, it seemed to young Dollie — the various familiar scenes as they drove through the streets of the town.

But she tensed visibly as they approached the family home on Main Street, and when they drove up she jammed on the brakes so violently that her daughter had to brace herself to keep from lurching forward.

An instant later, however, Mrs. Feagan relaxed. Armed with a short-handled rake, 81-year-old Viola King was raking rubbish into a small bonfire with a vigour remarkable for her years.

Relieved to see her alive and so energetic, Mrs. Feagan and Dollie leapt from the car and ran to embrace her.

Happily the three women entered the house. There, spurning offers of help, the old lady served her visitors tea and cake. She always made tea for herself and her semi-invalid bachelor brother in mid-afternoon, but today Will Griswold had been taken for a drive by her eldest son, Sam. She had decided to stay at home to tidy the garden.

Over their teacups, grandmother, mother and daughter chatted. Gradually Mrs. Feagan's fear evaporated.

But it returned in full measure at a scream from her mother. Suddenly paling, Viola King was gasping for breath and trembling. A moment later she sagged to the floor, her face contorted in pain.

Panic-stricken, the two were at her side in an instant. Together they lifted her gently onto the couch. Then, while her mother rushed to the kitchen for a glass of water, Dollie made for the phone and called Dr. Edward McCreight, an old friend of the family and a schoolmate of Mrs. Feagan.

He arrived in less than five minutes, and was fumbling with his bag when the front door opened. The newcomer was Mrs. Lottie Dansby, the plump, kindly-looking next-door neighbour and tenant of Viola King.

"Heard a scream and saw the doctor's car pulling up, so I hurried over," she said in a hushed whisper to Mrs. Feagan. "Looks like she's took real bad." And then, with the easy assurance of one who has helped in many a sick room, she stepped over to the sofa and began rubbing the old woman's hands.

A brief examination was enough to send Dr. McCreight to the telephone to summon an ambulance. When he returned to his patient he noted that she had found a moment of respite from the convulsions which had been racking her. Frowning, he clapped his hands together loudly. Immediately, Mrs. King was gripped by another violent spasm. The doctor nodded his head gravely as Mrs. King gave a final shudder and then lay still.

At a signal from the doctor, Mrs. Dansby led the sobbing Feagans to the kitchen for coffee. With the women out of earshot, McCreight phoned Chief Deputy Bill Dunwody.

The officer, lank and mild-looking, with a weather-beaten face, lost no time in getting to the scene. After describing the old woman's death, the doctor told him, "I'm afraid we're going to have an autopsy performed on Mrs. King. She was poisoned; I'm almost certain of it. I can't say definitely, but it looks like strychnine. I tried the loud-noise test on her, and she responded to the sound. That's a fairly reliable test, in which anyone who has been subjected to the poison reacts violently to loud noises. But it will take an autopsy to establish for sure that strychnine was administered."

Dunwody immediately phoned Sheriff Jim Lee Gordon. Next he put in a call to the office of County Attorney Gilbert Smith, who turned out to be away on business. And finally he telephoned District Attorney Otis Miller.

Gordon and Miller were there in half an hour, and by dusk they had completed a preliminary investigation. Mrs. Dansby had washed the crockery the women had been using when the tragedy occurred. However, as Dunwody pointed out, the strychnine must have been administered earlier in the day.

To avoid alerting the killer, the officers decided to keep the nature of Mrs. King's death a secret if possible, at least until after the autopsy.

Their discussion was interrupted by the opening of the front door. Will Griswold and his nephew, Sam King, had returned.

"Is anything wrong?" Griswold asked anxiously.

"I'm afraid so," Dunwody said quietly. "Grandma King's dead. And we've got reason to believe that she was murdered."

Griswold said nothing. He stroked the back of a chair, with trembling hands. Sam King looked in shock, the colour fading from his cheeks, and his mouth tightening.

"Who on earth could have done it?" he demanded. "And why?"

"That's something we'll have to find out," Gordon replied. "But of one thing you can rest assured: we're not giving up until we do."

"I'm sure of that," Sam King murmured. "Meanwhile, if there's anything I can do ..."

"There is," Gordon replied. After informing him of the decision to keep the murder a secret within the family, the sheriff told him that they wanted his permission to perform an autopsy.

The word "autopsy" seemed to jolt the eldest son, but with obvious reluctance he acceded.

As the officers were about to depart, a new green

saloon pulled up and a tall, bulky man of about 45 hopped out. It was John King, the second of Grandma King's five sons. His expression was too composed for that of a man who had received bad news; obviously he hadn't yet heard.

As the investigators headed for a meeting with the county attorney, all three felt that it was hard to believe that Grandma King was really dead. Thin and wiry, her hair pulled tightly back from a face hollowed by the years, she was one of the wealthiest women in the district — and one of the most popular. Widowed in 1915 on the death of her rancher husband, by wise investments in land she had turned the money he had left her into a sizeable estate.

At the meeting with Smith, the county attorney, it was decided that on the following morning Dunwody would stand by at the hospital for the results of the autopsy. Smith would go to the bank and check on the recent transactions affecting Mrs. King's account, and the sheriff would question the Kings.

Saturday morning was a busy time at the First National Bank of Anson, and Smith had to wait a few minutes until George Evans, the president of the bank, was free. Evans expressed shock at the news that Grandma King was dead. "But I guess we can't live for ever," he said.

Explaining that he was there for a routine check on the dead woman's finances, Smith said that he wanted to have a look at Mrs. King's account ledgers for the past few months. Within a few minutes he was inspecting them.

A quick glance at the sheet for the month of March made the county attorney blink. Within 20 days, three cheques, each for more than $300, had been charged against the account, notwithstanding the fact that the frugal old lady's entire monthly expenditures rarely exceeded $100.

Asked to whose order the draft had been made payable, the bank president produced the cancelled cheques. All three were made out to cash, and all three had been endorsed by Mrs. Lottie Dansby.

"You sure the signatures are all valid?" Smith asked.

Evans compared them hurriedly with the specimens in the account file. "Positive," he replied. "Besides, Lottie Dansby may be the town gossip, but I doubt that she's a bold-faced forger."

Smith reached for his hat. "Nor do I," he said with a shrug. "And I'm sure I'll be able to get a satisfactory explanation from Mrs. Dansby when I drop by to see her."

Meanwhile Sheriff Gordon had arrived at the King home. He was met at the door by Mrs. Feagan, who proceeded to tell him the story of her nightmares.

The sheriff heard her out in attentive silence. "You certain it was only the dreams that brought you here?" he asked when she had finished.

"There hadn't been any talk or rumours of your mother dying or being seriously ill?" Mrs. Feagan shook her head. "I hadn't heard a word from anyone about her being sick."

Gordon got up. "I may have to call on you again, but if I do, I'm sure you'll understand."

Mrs. Feagan nodded. "Of course," she said. "And now if you'll excuse me, there are things I've got to see to regarding Mother's funeral."

As soon as she had gone, Smith appeared from the hallway where he had been waiting. He told the sheriff what he had discovered at the bank.

"The stubs in Mrs. King's cheque book might indicate what the money was for," the sheriff suggested. "Supposing we have a look at it."

The cheque book being duly produced from the top drawer of Grandma King's old-fashioned desk, Smith began riffling through the stubs. To his astonishment, he discovered that none of the cheques had been recorded.

Gordon motioned to the door. "Maybe Lottie Dansby has the answers," he said. "Let's go find out."

A single jab of the front bell of the small white cottage occupied by Lottie Dansby and her husband brought the plump little woman bustling to the door. Greeting the officers warmly, she waved them inside and saw them comfortably seated.

"Real neighbourly of you to drop by, Sheriff," she said, beaming broadly. "It's the first time I've had the pleasure."

Embarrassed, Gordon took a little time clearing his throat. "I'm afraid we're here on business. We want you to explain how three large cheques of Mrs. King's happen to be carrying your endorsement."

Mrs. Dansby looked hurt. There was nothing to explain, she said. Mrs. King had been unable, because of her age, to get into town without some discomfort, and so had asked her to cash the cheques for her. And, naturally, she had been only too glad to oblige.

Gordon nodded. "Did she mention to you why she needed such large sums in cash?"

Mrs. Dansby shook her head. "To tell you the truth, I'm just as curious as you are. Once she did ask me not to mention to Mr. Griswold that I was going to the bank for her, but I don't think that meant anything in particular."

Recalling the absence of stubs for the cheques, Smith asked if Mrs. Dansby could account for this. She couldn't. In her opinion, she said, it merely emphasised the old lady's desire for secrecy.

The officers got up to go, and Mrs. Dansby accompanied them to the door. "I do hope you're not going to be hard on the children, Sheriff," she said feelingly. "Maybe they could all use the money they're going to come into, but just the same, I'm positive that none of them had anything to do with Mrs. King's death."

It was only then that Gordon recalled that Mrs. Dansby had been present when Grandma King died. He warned her not to mention the nature of her death to anyone.

"I haven't breathed a single word, and I won't," Mrs. Dansby replied. "You can count on that."

Outside, the sheriff asked the county attorney what Mrs. Dansby had meant about the King children needing money. As far as he knew, they were all doing well.

The door of the King home swung open abruptly and Dollie Feagan poked her head out. "Mr. Dunwody just phoned," she said. "He wants you to call him back. He's got some important news."

The autopsy had confirmed that Grandma King had died of strychnine poisoning. The lethal dose had been mixed with her food. But as she had eaten a fairly substantial lunch, and had possibly eaten again at some time during the afternoon, it was impossible to determine what the fatal dish had been.

The funeral was scheduled for 2 o'clock that afternoon, and it was respect, not duty, that led Gordon and Smith to the Baptist church where Grandma King's husband had been the first sexton.

Afterwards the investigators returned to the King homestead. Will Griswold answered the door. The sheriff mentioned the small bequest that had been left him. He didn't need the money, Griswold said with a wistful smile. It was a token more than anything else, and he was glad the children were provided for.

The officers thanked the old man and left the room to interview Sam King. They found him poring over papers at Grandma King's desk.

"They told me at the bank that your mother had cashed three large cheques totalling close to $1,000 within the past twenty days," said Smith.

"What on earth for?" Sam King demanded.

"Don't you know?"

King looked annoyed. "Of course I don't know."

"We thought maybe you would, as you've been given the power of attorney," Gordon told him.

"I've been busy lately, and I haven't had a chance to look into her affairs yet."

John King and two of his brothers had gone directly from the church to the other end of the county to return three elderly relatives to their homes, and weren't expected back until late that night. Meanwhile the investigators decided to try to track down the source of the strychnine.

They found that no registered poisons had been sold by any of nine local chemists for some time.

"I'm not surprised," Gordon shrugged. "I imagine that anyone who was fixing to get rid of somebody here in Anson wouldn't buy the poison in town. Probably go to Hamlin, Stamford, or Hawley for it. Let's drive over to Hamlin and see what we can turn up."

The Hamlin drugstores reported no sales of strychnine for five months. The investigators drove on to Stamford, 14 miles north of Anson, and pulled up in front of the City Drug Store. The assistant on duty produced a battered green ledger and flipped it open to the latest entries of registered poison sales.

Seeing the final entry on the page, the officers

stiffened. On April 2nd strychnine in the amount of 28 grains had been sold to an E. G. Bethany of Peacock, and April 2nd was the day that Grandma King had been murdered!

"E. G. Bethany, eh?" said the sheriff. "What do you know about him?"

"It wasn't a he, it was a she," the assistant replied. "I never saw her before in my life."

"What did she look like?"

"Nothing special. Black hair, fortyish, and kind of well filled out, as I recall. Now that you mention it, though, I remember that she seemed flustered when I told her that she'd have to sign for the poison. She made like to lay it down, and then all of a sudden she picked up the pen and signed."

If the woman purchasing the poison had been involved in the murder, E. G. Bethany would probably turn out to be a fictitious name. However, when the investigators consulted the Peacock directory, they were astonished to find that there was a listing for a Bethany. A minute later they were on their way to Peacock.

Mrs. Bethany herself answered their ring. Tall and pleasant-looking, she seemed completely bewildered when they explained their errand. In all her life she had never had any occasion to purchase poison, she said, and it had been more than a year since she had last set foot in Stamford. Furthermore she was ready and willing to accompany the officers back to the drugstore so that the assistant could have a look at her.

Asked if she knew Grandma King, she replied that she did, adding that she was shocked to hear of her death. She had formerly lived in Anson, she went on, and she still kept up with some of her old friends there — the Bill Fosters, the Sam Mercers, the Jordans, the Dansbys ..."

"Lottie Dansby?"

The woman nodded. "That's right," she said. "Lottie and I are pretty close. As a matter of fact, poor old Lottie used to live here in Peacock."

The officers hastened back to Anson. A brand-new blue saloon was standing in the driveway of the Dansby cottage when they arrived. Lottie Dansby didn't delay answering the door. As before, she gave them a cordial reception and ushered them back into her tidy parlour.

"That's a handsome-looking car out there in the driveway," said the sheriff. "Whose is it?"

"Why, it's mine, sheriff," Mrs. Dansby replied. "It's brand-new."

"So I noticed," Gordon replied. "Mind telling me what you paid for it?"

"A little less than $1,000. Thinking of buying one, sheriff?"

"No, I wasn't," Gordon replied. "I was thinking that that's just about what those three cheques you cashed for Mrs. King came to."

Mrs. Dansby sat bolt upright. "I don't know what you mean," she shrilled. "Exactly what are you driving at?"

"Merely this — that you killed Grandma King. There's a drugstore clerk over in Stamford who is ready to identify you as the woman who purchased 28 grains of strychnine yesterday morning and palmed herself off as 'E. G. Bethany.' For your information, we've spoken to Mrs. Bethany and ..."

A quiver ran suddenly through Lottie Dansby's plump frame, and she began weeping hysterically. Through her tears she sobbed out her confession.

She had got her near-sighted victim to sign three blank cheques under the impression that they were receipts for payments of house and garage-rents given her at the time.

When Lottie Dansby had learned that Mrs. King had given her son the power of attorney, she had decided to act, knowing that he would soon be checking his mother's accounts. After returning home from Stamford with the poison, she had mixed it in a glass of ice-cold lemonade. Then, spotting the old lady working in the garden shortly after lunch, she had handed her the lethal cooler, seeing to it that Mrs. King drank it in her presence.

Just over a month after Grandma King died in agony, Lottie Dansby went on trial for murder. Two days later, on May 12th, she was convicted. After several delays, in which the "good neighbour" appealed for another trial, Mrs. Dansby began serving her sentence of life imprisonment.

But what induced Mrs. Feagan's nightmare was never explained, as in the next story when a mother, living in south east London, had dreams that were to solve her son's murder.

Lottie Dansby. Ice-cold lemonade and strychnine

6

... MORE DREAMS, MORE MURDER
SOUTH EAST LONDON, SEPTEMBER 1923

Their son had been missing for many months now, and they desperately missed him. "You know, Gordon, I had that dream again last night, it was terrible," Mrs. Tombe said in a choked voice. Her husband, the Rev. George Gordon Tombe, took her hand and tried to reassure her.

Breakfast in their house in Wells Park Road, Sydenham, in south-east London had become fraught since the dreams had started. In the opinion of Mr. Tombe it had all become a nightmare, and he was rightly concerned about his wife's health.

"I didn't want to tell you, Gordon," his wife confessed, "but it is something I must share. I feel something ought to be done about it." She paused before adding, "It was so vivid, and I remember each detail so distinctly, I'm scared. I think we should do something, tell someone."

He reached across the breakfast table and held one of her hands in his.

"The police, my dear?"

She bit her under-lip, and nodded in a jerky, tense motion. "Yes. I've thought about it, Gordon. I think you should go to Scotland Yard. I really do."

She withdrew her hand, and her husband said, "Tell me what you dreamed last night."

His wife took some moments to compose herself before she said, "Well, it wasn't quite the same last night. I saw Eric again, but this time he wasn't trying to tell me something. He was very still. He was dead."

When she hesitated her husband asked, "Do you know where he was?"

"Yes," she replied. "At the bottom of a well. I'm sure he's been murdered, Gordon. I've never been so sure of anything in my whole life."

The fierceness with which she uttered the last words brought a frown to the husband's face.

"Very well, my dear," he said calmly. "I will pay a visit to Scotland Yard and ask them to find Eric for us." He leaned back in his chair. "Perhaps then you won't have this dream worry you again."

This was the reason that took the Reverend Gordon Tombe, a priest of the Church of England, to Scotland Yard in the late summer of 1923. He made known his business and was shown into a room where he met a man who looked more like his conception of a barrister than a detective.

"I am Superintendent Carlin, Mr. Tombe, how can I help you?"

Across the width of a table littered with papers the visitor from Sydenham told the superintendent about his wife's recurring dream, in which her son appeared as though he wished to warn her about some disaster.

"And now, Mr. Carlin, she has seen him lying at the bottom of a well. She is convinced that is where his body will be found."

"At the bottom of a well?"

"Yes."

"Where does he live?"

"Well, he lived at Kenley until there was a fire. We haven't heard from him for some time."

"Is there a well on the property?" Carlin inquired.
The troubled face above the clerical collar moved slowly from side to side.

"I really don't know. Eric certainly never mentioned one to his mother or to me."

Carlin's fingers drummed on the table top for several seconds before he said, "Mr. Tombe, I think you'd better tell me all you know about your son's recent activities."

He was told how George Eric Gordon Tombe, the clergyman's son, had always been fond of horses and riding. During the recent war he had met a suave, smooth-talking character named Ernest Dyer who had discussed plans for opening some stables. The two men had remained friendly, and after they had been demobbed Dyer called on the younger man and told him he had heard of a stud farm in Surrey being up for sale.

Eric Tombe's mother and father had found little attraction in the proposition, but their son had accepted with enthusiasm the chance to become Dyer's partner. He helped to raise £5,000, the place was purchased, and Dyer the businessman of the partnership promptly paid the first premium on an insurance of £12,000.

The stud farm was situated in Kenley, and its previous owner, who sold it to Dyer, was Percy Woodland, a trainer who had moved to bigger things in his career. The new owners moved into their property, and almost at once Dyer revealed a surprising passion for cars, one which took him away from The Welcomes Stud Farm for lengthy spells, while the inexperienced Eric Tombe was left to battle alone with the problem of training horses.

Not surprisingly, the partners found themselves disagreeing about their investment and their business interests. The venture was doomed to eventual failure. It could only be a question of time before young Tombe admitted the truth he did not wish to see clearly.

In April, 1921, while Tombe was away from the farm it was badly damaged by fire. Dyer had lost little time in putting in his claim to the insurance company, which sent an investigator to review the damaged property. They had refused to pay the claim. Tombe had expected his partner to sue, but Dyer had no stomach for pressing his claim in a court of law. The fire fiasco had been the beginning of the end for the curious partnership. A year passed in fruitless argument, and almost on the anniversary of the fire Dyer and Eric Tombe ended their association. Dyer had left, and the clergyman had not heard from his son since receiving a letter dated April 17th, 1922. "I shall be coming to see you on Saturday," it said, but of course, he never arrived.

Another year had passed, and the missing Eric Tombe's mother started to have bad dreams about her son, in which he appeared to pass on a warning of some kind which she could not understand.

"Let me have the address of your son's bank, Mr. Tombe," Carlin said when the clergyman came to the end of his story, "and also the addresses of any friends of his known to you."

When he had written them down he rose and shook hands with the unhappy father. "If I have news you'll hear from me, Mr. Tombe," he promised.

The clergyman returned to Sydenham.

Carlin lost no time in contacting the manager of the West End bank where Eric Tombe had an account. He was provided with information that struck him as most significant. For instance, in April, 1922, the missing Eric Tombe's current account held a useful balance of more than £2,500. However, at the end of that same month a letter from him conveyed instructions for £1,350 to be transferred to the bank's branch in Paris, with the request that arrangements be made for Ernest Dyer to draw on it with no limit. Dyer's specimen signature was enclosed with the request.

Eric Tombe's signature had not been questioned, and the instructions had been accepted. Throughout May and June, Dyer had drawn on the Paris balance, and in July the West End branch received additional instructions to allow Dyer to draw on the balance remaining in London.

Carlin had the two letters containing instructions to the bank produced and he signed for them. Before he left the manager's office he had been told of something that had perturbed the bank's officials. Dyer had made a trip to the West Country and there overdrawn the Tombe account. He had been handing out cheques which could not be honoured.

Among the addresses left with Carlin by the missing Eric Tombe's father was one of a young woman who had been a friend of both partners in The Welcomes venture. He paid her a visit and was told she hadn't seen the younger man for a year and a half. She related an incident which had puzzled her at the time.

With a friend and the two stud farm partners she had agreed to a short holiday trip to Paris. They agreed to meet on April 25th and take the boat train. The two young women were on time, and Dyer arrived late and alone, but with a telegram he said Eric Tombe had sent him, apologising for having to go "overseas" at very short notice.

So Paris was out.

What had puzzled the young woman interviewed

by Carlin was not the calling off of the trip but Eric Tombe's use of the word "overseas" in his telegram. He had apparently had to go to France before, and whenever he had spoken to her he had always said France, and she couldn't remember him using the soldier's word "overseas." Somehow it struck her as being wrong.

She told Carlin she hadn't seen Dyer for about nine months, when she had heard he was going to the north of England. She did not know where or why he was making the trip. Carlin had inquiries made, but could not learn of anyone seeing Dyer in London after going north. It was important to trace Dyer, for he was the only person with a first-hand story of where Eric Tombe had vanished. So Carlin had a general inquiry sent to police forces in the north of England.

The routine inquiry produced evidence of a mysterious fatal shooting in the November of the previous year, 1922. The report had been handed in by a Detective Inspector Abbott, who had been on the trail of a number of worthless cheques. A man named Fitzsimmons had been a free spender and had talked loud and long in bars and saloons along the Yorkshire coast. He had also put a few advertisements in local papers, advising men of the highest integrity to apply to him for details of employment with very bright prospects.

"Of the highest integrity" had been his own choice of words. Inspector Abbott decided a newcomer to the Yorkshire coastal resorts, who behaved as though he had money to burn could bear investigation. Moreover, one detail of the advertisement for men of the highest integrity had roused the detective's suspicions. Apparently the highest integrity was not enough. Each applicant was to be interviewed in person by Mr. Fitzsimmons, and the interview would take place only if the applicant was able to produce a cash deposit.

For a man who had been littering Yorkshire with dud cheques the request for cash looked to the inspector like a desperate attempt to line lean pockets.

Abbott called on Fitzsimmons at the Bar Hotel in Scarborough where the advertiser was staying. A visit from the police obviously took Fitzsimmons by surprise. He appeared unconcerned, but agreed to take the inspector to his room, where they could talk.

He didn't reach his room. On the way Abbott saw Fitzsimmons sneak a hand to his pocket, and the inspector decided the other had some incriminating papers he wished to destroy, and threw himself on his companion.

The two men collided against the wall, fell to the ground struggling, and Abbott was suddenly checked by the sound of a gunshot and the man under him going limp.

Fitzsimmons had not been reaching for incriminating papers as Abbott supposed, but for a revolver. In the dead man's room Abbott came upon a gambler's eyeshade and a mask, some soldier's service medals, and a badge from a branch of the British Legion. The case in which he found these personal effects had the initials E.T. stencilled on the side. It also held nearly 200 blank cheques, on which had been pencilled the name of Eric Gordon Tombe. To Abbott it looked as though the pencilled name had been traced, and was there to be inked over at leisure. Some items of a personal nature, the property of this Eric Gordon Tombe, were found in the bag.

Fitzsimmons had obviously been a crook, and Abbott was sure the name was bogus. He started his own inquiry, and learned that Fitzsimmons was actually a certain Ernest Dyer. He was wanted for passing a stream of rubber cheques in the West Country, and was currently sought by the police in Gloucestershire and Herefordshire.

Now some 10 months later Carlin finished reading the curious report that appeared to end his own inquiry before it had properly begun. Dyer had come to the end of his tether. Carrying that revolver had been the last resort of a desperate man.

But what of Eric Tombe?

Carlin decided it was time to visit The Welcomes at Kenley. He had not been unduly impressed by the story of the dream related by the clergyman's wife. In his line of business dreams were not evidence enough. Any detective prepared to admit himself impressed by one would be endangering his career.

But the fire at the stud farm, the refusal of an insurance company to pay up, and the desperate last resort of Ernest Dyer pointed to a sequence of events that might need investigating. Especially at the stud farm where the two men invested their money and where the fire took place.

Kenley is a few miles south of Croydon and in the 1920s it was very much in the country.

Carlin arranged to be met by Detective Inspector Hedges, and the two men arrived at the ruins of The Welcomes on a bright September day in 1923 and had to cut back the weeds choking a five-barred gate leading to the property.

The place was utterly derelict. Paths were overgrown and choked, brickwork of outbuildings and stables was crumbling badly, and the charred remains of the badly damaged house smelled of decay and stale embers, with a pervasive odour of damp. When the police had forced entry into the locked ruin they found little for their trouble. The place had obviously not been lived in for many months. There was a small cottage on the property. They broke into this. Again they found nothing to explain why or when the property had been deserted.

Carlin tramped the limits of the farm, and came upon five wells or cess-pits. Suitable drainage had obviously been a problem.

"I'll want these wells examined, Hedges," Carlin told the divisional man.

Inspector Hedges appeared surprised.

"What do you expect to find, sir?" he asked, obviously puzzled by the request.

"I'm not sure."

Constables in gumboots and shirt-sleeves began clearing the vegetation and slabs of broken concrete from the first of the dried-up wells. By the time they had cleared two of the pits and assured Carlin they held nothing of interest for the Yard man the September day was dying.

"What do we do now, sir?" asked Hedges, aware that his men were tired after their exertions.

"Let the men rest, then start on number three," Carlin told him.

Hurricane lanterns were lit, and the heaving policemen began tearing away the weeds and knee-high grasses choking the mouth of the third well. When the weeds had been cleared they found more rubble blocking the pit.

Obviously someone had been careful to fill in all the pits, which seemed a curious waste of time, for it had been work that served no useful purpose except, perhaps, to discourage anyone from searching.

It was an eerie scene under the trees beyond the gutted farmhouse, where the lanterns threw long, wildly gyrating shadows over the ground and up among the tree branches. In the distance birds alarmed by the activity kept up an inquisitive chatter. But even their sharp sounds fell silent at last, and as Carlin and Hedges stood there in the autumn night the only sounds were the sharp impact of spade on stone and the deep, harsh breathing of the heaving constables.

The work was arduous and tricky, for under the rubble of broken concrete and brick was a pile of loose earth. There had been no loose earth in the previous two wells. The discovery excited Carlin. He knew why someone filling in a well might use such packing.

To conceal an offensive odour.

The loose earth became mud, and the thick ooze was dredged out a spadeful at a time, and then one of the constables began coughing. The other swore.

"What's the matter?" asked Inspector Hedges, stepping forward.

"It stinks, sir, and there's water down there," one of the diggers told him.

A bucket was lowered on a rope and the well drained until the bucket was scraping up thick, viscous mud again. Carlin told the men to stand back, and he picked up one of the lanterns and held it down in the mouth of the well. A heavy fetid stench rose in his face. He narrowed his eyes, twisting the lantern in his hands until the light reached the bottom of the smelly pit.

He saw something protruding from the slimy ooze that made him hold his breath.

He thought of a woman unable to rest easy during long nights in Sydenham while she worried about her missing son. A mother who had dreamed of her son's body being at the bottom of a well.

Carlin stood back, passed the lantern to Hedges.

"Take a look," he invited.

The divisional inspector took Carlin's place and peered down the shaft of the well among the dancing shadows. He straightened abruptly.

"A body's been stuffed down there head first," he said, his voice tense. "That's a foot sticking up."

"I want the men to be very careful how they remove the body," Carlin said gravely.

Extracting the body from the obnoxious ooze and raising it from the well required not only patience and time but the exercise of considerable ingenuity. At length, however, the men hauling on the ropes slippery with stinking mud were able to get their hands on the legs. The clothed body of a young man was deposited on the pile of springy weeds at the side of the well.

Hedges came and stood beside Carlin, who said in a quiet voice, "There'll be no need to empty the other two wells, inspector."

As the men cleaned up, Carlin made arrangements with Hedges to have the post-mortem examination completed without delay.

A few hours later Carlin received the police surgeon's report. The body taken from the well was that of a man of Tombe's approximate age, who had been shot at close range with a sporting gun.

The crime was now clear in Carlin's mind. Dyer had been broke and with no prospect of obtaining fresh funds except by robbing his partner in the stud farm. His arson plot had been a mere bluff that had been called when the insurance company refused to pay his claim. He had not gone to court because he knew very well that his past, as well as his fire claim, would not stand close investigation.

To rob his partner meant Dyer had first to remove young Tombe permanently. Murder had been the only way out. A fatal accident would have been too risky. So the clergyman's son had been killed when Dyer pressed the trigger of his gun, and the body had been dumped in one of the wells. All five were filled in as a precaution two months later.

Then Dyer had left to start drawing on his murdered partner's credit at the bank. He thought he had been clever, but he had been a fool. He had made no provision for the time when the credit ran dry except to go on using bogus cheques.

He had realised the truth. His wartime revolver had been carried because he knew he might have to use it. He couldn't be sure that one day the middle well of the five at The Welcomes would not be cleared and its grisly secret laid bare.

When Inspector Abbott announced that he was a police officer who would like to ask Fitzsimmons some questions in the privacy of his room Dyer had jumped to the wrong conclusion.

He had thought Abbott was about to arrest him for murder.

So Ernest Dyer had kept one jump ahead of the law, but it proved to be the one really long jump that men of violence had feared for a great many years. He had decided on the quick way out. His conscience had made him a coward.

But none of this incredible drama would be told in a court of law. Indeed, the actual pattern of bold deceit and brutal conniving would never have been revealed, most likely, if a dead man's mother had not been troubled at night by a dream that to her was vividly rational and terribly true.

Carlin, before his retirement from Scotland Yard, arrested a number of notorious killers, but he tackled no case with such ironic values as that of Ernest Dyer, the killer who couldn't face arrest.

At the eventual inquest on the remains brought from the stud farm the Reverend Gordon Tombe had to perform a public duty which won him the sympathy of all who read the story in the newspapers. He was taken into a bare room and shown a sheeted form. The sheet was lowered from a sunken face topped with familiar curly hair. He looked at the stained clothes, the wrist-watch, the tie-pin, and the cuff links worn by the dead man.

He did not have to look at the hole in the back of the head where four lead slugs had entered to reach his son's brain.

The shocked clergyman told the coroner in a hoarse whisper that the remains he had viewed were those of his son Eric Gordon Tombe.

The young woman Carlin had interviewed earlier was called to give evidence, and she appeared with a veil over her bowed head and dressed in black. She had a story to tell that was a vital part of the case Carlin had pieced together.

She had admitted telling Dyer she did not believe Eric Tombe had sent the telegram announcing he had been called overseas. Half in earnest, half trying to get a reaction from Dyer, she had said, "I think you've done away with him."

Dyer had gaped at her.

She had gone on, "If you don't tell me what you know, I'm going to the police and they can make inquiries."

Dyer found his voice. Giving her a tight grin, he had said, "We'll go together."

"What about giving them a ring now?" she had suggested. Dyer had gone down like a pricked balloon.

"Do that and I might as well blow my brains out," he said.

She had been shocked by the admission and suddenly saw that if she carried out her threat she might become responsible for Dyer's death. That was something she had no wish to live with.

When she stood down the pattern of the case was complete.

Moreover, as her evidence at the inquest had shown, the girl was someone Dyer should have avoided. She had told the coroner she had been engaged to Tombe, and so not unnaturally an unexpected act on the part of her fiancé — and one she considered out of character — had made her suspicious of Dyer, especially as she had been made aware of a new coldness between the two men when they met one day in April 1922 in Tombe's Haymarket flat.

The coroner's jury returned a verdict of murder committed on approximately April 21st, 1922.

When Carlin walked out of the court the case that had resulted in no startling arrest, but which had made headlines and history alike, was over so far as the record was concerned. But Carlin himself felt he should at least pursue one additional line of inquiry that would have been open to him if he had still been seeking Eric Tombe's murderer.

Ernest Dyer had left a widow and Carlin called upon her, an interview recalled below in the detective's own words:

"In the course of that interview I got a most graphic description of a midnight scene at the cottage at The Welcomes, which had escaped the fire.

"It was on June 22nd, or exactly two months after Eric Tombe was murdered, that she was sitting alone in the cottage about eleven o'clock, when she suddenly heard the sound of stones dropping against the drain-pipe.

"Dyer was away from home, so she thought. She believed him, in fact, to be at that moment in France. She called to her dog, and opened the front door. The moon was up, but there were a lot of big black clouds scudding across the sky and the yard was only lit fitfully with an alternate silvery light and complete shadow.

"She peered out, and her dog began to growl and his hairs to bristle. Then the animal gave a savage bark and dashed forward to a disused cowshed in the corner of the yard and he flew at someone who was concealed in the shadows there.

"A moment later, to her astonishment, she saw that it was her husband. He came out into the yard, and as he did so the moonlight shone full on his face. She saw that he was deathly pale and was trembling all over. When he spoke it was with great agitation. 'What are you doing here, Ernest?' she asked him. 'I thought you were miles away.'

"With his teeth chattering, in spite of the fact that it was a mild June night, he answered: 'You know the state of my credit. I don't want to be seen near here in the daylight.'

"Mrs. Dyer stepped out into the yard and started to walk towards her husband. In great excitement he held up his hands and cried: 'Don't come over here. Don't come out. Get into the house again for God's sake.'

"But, as Carlin concluded, the full significance of Dyer's attitude, the reason for his secret midnight visit to The Welcomes, was not understood by his wife till the body of Eric Gordon Tombe was found."

And when Carlin left the widow he was convinced that Mrs. Dyer had heard her husband while he was engaged in the task of filling in the five wells.

Later he had joined her, but he refused to offer

anything like a satisfactory explanation. After all, how could he explain to an obviously unsettled and frightened woman that he had been occupied in hiding a body?

Which in fact he had done quite successfully — but for a dream that haunted his victim's mother many months after both victim and murderer had died, both by violence, both by the same hand.

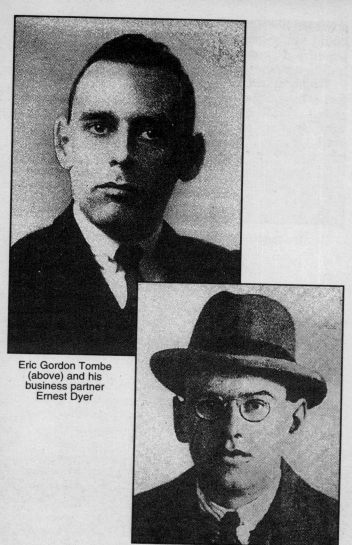

Eric Gordon Tombe
(above) and his
business partner
Ernest Dyer

The derelict Welcomes Stud Farm at Kenley in Surrey

7
THE BLUEBELLE ENIGMA
OFF THE BAHAMAS, NOVEMBER 12TH, 1961

You don't have to be old and wise to be able to see into the future. The uncanny gift can be possessed by a child, as pupils at a Wisconsin school discovered.

Alfred W. Dupperault, a well-to-do, 41-year-old Wisconsin optician, was taking his family on the trip of a lifetime. He was chartering a ketch to take them on a cruise to the Bahamas. The whole family were going: Alfred, his wife Jean, 38, and their children — Brian, 14, Terry Jo, 11, and seven-year-old Renee. All were excited and looking forward to it, and Terry Jo's teacher shared that enthusiasm on behalf of her young pupil at Wequiock School near the family's Green Bay home in Wisconsin.

But the teacher, Janet Wieting, was surprised by something in a note she received from Terry Jo. The letter was addressed to "Miss Wieting and the Rest of the Class," and in it Terry Jo wrote: "I am now sure that we will never come back."

Meanwhile the family's holiday arrangements were being finalised. Through a boating agency, Alfred Dupperault corresponded with Harold Pegg of Hollywood, Florida, owner of the 60-foot ketch *Bluebelle*, arranging to charter the vessel at $100 a day.

As Dupperault closed the deal, it was the ketch's

44-year-old skipper who particularly impressed him. When he first saw Julian Harvey he immediately felt sure that here was a man in whom he could have complete confidence. True, Harvey stammered slightly, but he was a former Air Force lieutenant-colonel and a well-known yachtsman in Florida boating circles.

"And how about that good-looking wife of his?" said Dupperault, nudging his own wife.

Mary Dene Harvey, 34, was a russet-haired former airline stewardess. She could whip up a meal or swab down a deck with equal skill and alacrity. Julian Harvey had been introduced to the sleek, well-groomed girl as she sunbathed on the patio of Miami's DuPont Plaza Hotel two years before, Dupperault learned. They were married in July, 1961, in Mexico.

"An ideal couple and an ideal crew," Dupperault thought contentedly as the ketch moved out to sea on November 8th, 1961, from the harbour at Fort Lauderdale.

Four breathless, exhilarating days of sun and sea followed, as the ketch roamed from horizon to horizon, a speck on the ocean's vastness. The Dupperaults and the Harveys became friends; they swam, skin-dived and lobster-fished. The children found their sea legs and rejoiced in the sway of the deck as *Bluebelle* was lifted by long, low rollers of the sparkling Atlantic.

Harvey nosed the ketch into the bay of the sleepy settlement of Sandy Point on Great Abaco Island for a few hours. The islanders waved at the holiday-makers and the Dupperaults waved back, fascinated by the isle so different from their native woods and lakes. Green Bay, now bracing itself for the white Wisconsin winter, was indeed far away.

On November 12th *Bluebelle* cast off and the family faced the sea again with pleasurable anticipation. The ketch returned to the ocean as a bird to the sky. The trade winds were fair, and course was set for the North-West Providence Channel, north of Nassau. As she sped on *Bluebelle's* masts cast lengthening shadows over her deck and the velvet darkness closed in.

From the north the next morning steamed the *Gulflion*, an oil tanker bound for Puerto Rico. With increasing light, visibility from her bridge improved. The mate on watch, John Huval, paced behind his wheelhouse windows and scanned the sea ahead.

A seaman, Dennis Gochenour, gazed moodily at the monotonous waves. Suddenly he blinked. Something was out there, bobbing up and down in the swells. He looked again, then yelled to the bridge: "There's a man out there in a dinghy! He's waving to us!"

The mate swung his binoculars in the direction indicated by Gochenour. He gave crisp orders. Soon the heavy tanker was slowing and drawing close to the man adrift. They saw that he was tall and had light-coloured hair. He wore khaki trousers and a faded sports shirt. A life-raft was lashed to the dinghy.

"Help!" the man shouted. "I have a dead baby with me!"

A small, still form lay at the man's feet. A line was swiftly tossed to the dinghy and the seamen watched as it was secured to the little vessel's bow in professional fashion. A basket was lowered to pick up the dead child. The man in the dinghy followed up a ladder thrown over the tanker's side.

The *Gulflion's* skipper, Captain Oscar Verkouille, faced the man questioningly. He seemed to be in a daze. "I'm very grateful to you for picking me up," he said. "My name is Julian Harvey. I was skipper of a ketch called *Bluebelle*—" Then, with a catch of breath, he added, "She caught fire and sank last night."

"Anyone else aboard her besides you and this little girl?" Captain Verkouille asked.

Harvey nodded. "My wife — and the five passengers — are gone." He spoke slowly, calmly. He added: "It will get me in a little while."

A sailor handed him a cigarette. Harvey inhaled deeply. Then he said: "A sudden squall came up and hit the ketch. It snapped the mainmast off about one-third of its length up. The mast fell, bringing the mizzen-mast with it, turning the deck into a shambles. The mainmast section went into the bottom of the ketch like an arrow — she had an inch and three-quarter wooden hull — and she didn't stand a chance. She was just a hulk wallowing in the sea.

"Then fire broke out. I couldn't get to the passengers or my wife through the flames. The ketch was going down — I had no choice but to get into her dinghy. I got away from her and saw the child floating in the water. I pulled her into the dinghy, but she was dead."

He said he thought that "several" of those on board had been killed when the mainmast snapped and had plunged to the deck.

His listeners heard his tale in silence. As seamen, they realised the full horror of Harvey's story. Quietly, they led him below decks and served him a meal.

Harvey named all who had been on board the ill-fated *Bluebelle*, writing down the names for Captain Verkouille. He seemed unable to remember the name of the dead girl he had picked up. But an hour later his memory returned. "She was Renee Dupperault," he said. "I think she was seven years old."

Captain Verkouille radioed his news to the Coast Guard at Miami. Within minutes a message was returned. "Proceed at once to Nassau," the nearest port of any size.

"We had no charts for that trip," Captain Verkouille recalled later. "But Harvey's knowledge of those waters was good enough."

The skipper of the lost *Bluebelle* talked more about the disaster during the four-hour journey to Nassau. A choking grief crept into his voice when he spoke of his dead wife.

In Nassau he repeated his story, this time to a calm, white-clad British naval officer, commander of the port. The officer listened impassively. When the account finished he rose and shook Julian Harvey's hand. "Well, I suppose everything possible has been done," he commented.

The body of little Renee was brought ashore. The British authorities decided to obtain a coroner's verdict on the cause of her death.

Julian Harvey returned to Miami and was immediately questioned by officers of the American Coast Guard Marine and Inspection Division. The investigation into the sinking of *Bluebelle* had begun.

Harvey told again of the sudden squall that had snapped the ketch's mainmast. On charts he pinned down the exact location of the tragedy: 50 miles north of Nassau, 120 miles east of Miami.

A slight discrepancy entered his account when compared with the one he had offered aboard the *Gulflion*. On the tanker he had said that some of those aboard *Bluebelle* had been killed when the mainmast toppled. To the Coast Guard he said: "The boat burst into flames and sank within fifteen minutes. I don't know what happened to the others on board. I last saw them going over the side. I was at the wheel and they were at the stern. I couldn't get to them. After I was in the water I managed to get into the dinghy."

Harvey said it was possible that Mrs. Dupperault and her son Brian "might have been injured" by the mast's fall. He did not mention death.

The Coast Guard scheduled a formal inquiry for November 27th.

Experienced yachtsmen, however, read the account in their newspapers — then read it again. There was something strange about a ketch of *Bluebelle's* class succumbing to a sudden squall in that fashion.

Harold Pegg, *Bluebelle's* owner, was worried. He had hired Julian Harvey on October 4th, 1961, as the vessel's skipper, to work its charter service for him. "That ketch," Harold Pegg said, "had twice as much fire protection as the Coast Guard requires."

At Toms River, New Jersey, the former owner of *Bluebelle*, an attorney named Harry Duckworth, could not understand it either. "I was amazed to read that the mast had snapped off," he said later. "I had the mast rebuilt myself and it would take a hurricane to knock it down."

Harvey took up residence in the Sandman Motel in Miami and secluded himself. He appeared dazed and depressed, his demeanour that of a stoic but bitterly bereaved man. He telephoned an old friend, a former Air Force colleague, James Boozer, now owner of a Miami advertising firm.

"He came to my home in a state of shock and depression from the loss of his wife and the Dupperault family," Mr. Boozer said. "Harvey was a man who'd had more than his share of trouble. I guess he was accident-prone. I said to him, 'Some people say that this isn't your day or this isn't your week — but this isn't your life, Harv.' "

Julian Harvey was indeed "accident-prone." He'd had at least four wives, and his second wife was killed with her mother in a car accident in April, 1949. They were passengers in a car being driven by Harvey. The wife, Joan, and her mother, Mrs. Myrtle Boylen, were drowned when the car hurtled through a bridge rail at Fort Walton Beach, Florida, and plunged into a culvert.

Harvey, then an Air Force lieutenant-colonel stationed at nearby Eglin Air Force Base, told police that he was thrown clear as the car made its dive, but the two women inside were trapped. Colonel Harvey, sole survivor of that tragedy, emerged unscathed.

While he was stationed at Eglin an Air Force plane he was flying crashed. Later, on a mission from Edwards Air Force Base, California, another plane he was flying came down. This time Harvey was severely injured and spent several months in hospital. The crash caused extensive injury to his back and resulted in his eventual medical discharge.

And the *Bluebelle* was not the only craft to have gone down under him. Once, while racing his 100-foot sloop *Valient* off Cuba in 1958, the vessel was suddenly enveloped in flames and sank rapidly. Harvey collected $40,000 in insurance.

Earlier, in 1955, his yacht *Torbatross* sank in Chesapeake Bay after ramming the marked, submerged hull of an old battleship placed there for aerial target practice. Harvey's son, Lance, two other men and Harvey were rescued by Navy helicopters. Harvey collected $14,000 insurance.

But his Air Force record was dazzling — one few could equal. He emerged from World War II and the

Korean War lavishly decorated. He held two Distinguished Flying Crosses and nine Air Medals. He flew on 29 raids in Europe and Africa in World War II and 114 in Korea as a fighter pilot.

In 1944 he had displayed his daring in one episode in particular. The B-24 bomber, it was claimed, was always breaking in two when ditched in water, often drowning its crew. The Air Force needed someone to help to prove or disprove this. Harvey volunteered. He and a co-pilot slammed one of the lumbering bombers down on the James River, Virginia. The plane promptly fell apart and Harvey was nearly drowned. He got an Air Medal for this action.

All this and more about his background was learned by those investigating the tragic loss of the *Bluebelle*.

A great sea and air search had been launched to locate any more survivors. Ships, planes and helicopters scoured a carefully plotted expanse of the ocean, thousands of square miles in extent. All ships in the area were alerted to be on the lookout for bodies or fragments of floating wreckage that might shed further light on *Bluebelle's* tragic end.

Meanwhile Terry Jo's eerie letter to her teacher had come to light with news of the Dupperault family's disappearance. The child may not have foreseen just what was to happen, but she clearly expected something terrible.

Little Renee Dupperault's body was returned to Green Bay. But 1,400 miles away from the saddened community, on the borderless ocean, an incredible turn in the *Bluebelle* mystery was approaching.

On November 16th, George Syndinos, a carpenter on the Greek freighter *Captain Theo*, gathered his tools and mounted the flying deck of his ship. A damaged bulkhead needed repair on this highest place of the vessel's bridge, a vantage point for lookouts in stormy weather.

The *Captain Theo's* original destination at its European departure port had been Montreal. But last-minute orders had altered this to Houston, Texas.

Syndinos worked steadily through the morning, occasionally glancing at the wind-whipped sea. As the lunch break approached he rose to his feet and stared out over the ocean from horizon to horizon. Suddenly, he stiffened. He strode to the deck rail, his weather-beaten face tense. Far off, bobbing among the waves, a little girl sat on a white raft, paddling the craft with her hands.

Syndinos yelled down to other members of the crew on the deck below. He pointed to the raft with the little girl. A seaman bounded up to the bridge and the churning wake of the freighter described an arc as the vessel veered closer to the raft.

Captain Stylianos Coutsodontis directed operations as seamen eagerly volunteered to rescue the child from the sea. Now they could see the girl clearly. She was slender and her blonde hair hung in matted strings about her face. She had seen the freighter and appeared to be paddling desperately to try to reach it.

She sat on the forward end of the 5-by-4-foot balsawood float, and now the crew of *Captain Theo* spotted a new and terrible hazard. Huge sharks were swimming between the raft and the freighter, their fins slicing the water like razors and their shadowy forms visible beneath the surface.

The seamen sprang to launch a lifeboat. Then they abandoned this, realising that the twisting ocean currents in the area would make it impossible to manoeuvre the lifeboat to the girl on the raft. With desperate haste they constructed a raft of their own, lashing together oil drums and lumber. Within minutes it was completed and launched.

The girl waved weakly to the men as they rowed towards her. Sometimes she disappeared from their view; the ocean swells were large and girl and raft small. But the sailors quickly reached the raft, and as they did so the little girl smiled feebly. Then she amazed them by giving the sign of misfortune — thumbs down.

The seamen gathered her up. At 11 a.m. she was lifted aboard the freighter *Captain Theo*. Then she collapsed.

A sailor gently carried her to a vacant cabin. There she was carefully placed on a bunk and, still in her water-soaked red slacks and white sweater, wrapped in blankets.

Two Americans were serving aboard the Greek merchantman — Franklin O'Grady and Richard Kappus. They were the only English-speaking members of the crew and were working their way back to the United States after a cycle tour of Europe. They went to the little girl's bedside.

She regained consciousness in a few minutes. They offered her orange juice and water, and she grasped at them eagerly. "Don't try to talk," said O'Grady. "Easy — easy does it."

The freighter's skipper sat by her bunk as the girl seemed to recover slowly. O'Grady then asked her her name.

"Terry Jo," she croaked, her tongue swollen, lips parched. "Terry Jo Dupperault, from Green Bay, Wisconsin."

Then she lapsed back into sign language to answer the next question: "How long have you been in the water?"

Terry Jo held up five fingers.

"Five days?"

She nodded.

The seamen stared at the girl, then at each other.
"Were you in a boat?"

Terry Jo nodded, and again when she was asked if her family had been with her.

"What happened to them?"

She pointed downwards.

Captain Coutsodontis tried to tell her that there was a chance that some other ship had picked them up. But Terry Jo shook her head and again pointed down.

No one attempted to question her about the accident. She was too weak to try to talk.

At 11.17 a.m. the *Captain Theo* flashed a radio message to the Coast Guard at Miami that a girl giving the name of Terry Jo Dupperault had been found alive at sea. Within minutes the Coast Guard radioed back that a helicopter was on its way to pick her up.

By the time the helicopter had covered the 85 miles from Miami to the freighter, Terry Jo had sunk into a deep sleep. The helicopter came in low and straight, then swung in a circle around the vessel. Its crew scanned the freighter's deck: there was no place to land. The pick-up would have to be made by cable winch. The helicopter hovered above the freighter like some giant insect. Slowly, a large basket was lowered from its belly to the ship's deck.

O'Grady gently awakened Terry Jo. "Can you make it a short way across the deck?" he asked her.

She smiled and nodded. But as soon as she reached the upper deck she collapsed again. Kappus picked her up and carried her to the basket. Terry Joe was strapped in securely and a seaman gave the signal to haul her up.

"She went right back to sleep when we got her in — didn't say a word," the pilot said. He pointed the helicopter towards Miami and flew back as quickly as possible.

At Miami, Terry Jo was rushed to Mercy Hospital. There her feet were found to be shrivelled from immersion in salt water. Her skin had been burned dangerously by the sun. The doctors who examined her said she was suffering from loss of fluid and her heartbeat was too fast because of shock. There was danger of pneumonia.

Dr. Franklin Verdon carried out a head-to-toe examination and announced that Terry Jo was in a critical condition. "But," he added, "I think she'll make it."

The Coast Guard immediately intensified its search for other members of the Dupperault family and for Julian Harvey's wife. The cutter *Travis* and an 82-foot patrol boat hunted that night in the area where Terry Jo had been picked up. Two planes joined the search at daybreak. The Coast Guard had hitherto all but given up hope that any more survivors of the ketch *Bluebelle* would be found. The rescue of Terry Jo inspired fresh hope.

Under sedatives and on a glucose diet, Terry Jo gained strength rapidly. She began to smile and the fiery red of her skin gradually faded to a gentler hue.

Among the investigators intrigued by the sinking of *Bluebelle* a tense conversation took place. A telephone was lifted and an order given. A police guard appeared outside Terry Jo's room. The officers were discreet and polite. But they never left the flaxen-haired girl's door.

Inside the room, Dr. Verdon chatted with his young patient. Terry Jo's golden hair had returned to its natural softness. It was tied with a bright ribbon brought to her by nurses. "Tell me, Terry Jo," the doctor asked, "could you stretch out on that little raft?"

"No," she replied. "I just sat down."

"While you were out there, did you see any ships go by?"

"No. I saw a lot of planes."

"Was there anything you could do — like waving a handkerchief or something?"

"I waved my arms."

Julian Harvey at first knew nothing of the rescue of Terry Jo. The preliminary investigation of *Bluebelle's* loss had kept him busy; the Coast Guard had a lengthy report to make and many details were required that necessitated his help. The Coast Guardsmen wanted to know everything about the lost ketch from stem to stern, topmast to keel. They summoned the owner and asked Harvey to come along too. Pegg turned up with his attorney.

In an adjoining office sat Captain Barber, head of the Miami Inspection Division. His telephone rang.

The chief of the Sea and Rescue Branch of the Coast Guard's 7th District was on the line "Little girl from *Bluebelle* has been found," he said matter-of-factly. "She's going to live. Great, huh?" The caller went on to say, "Let me talk to Harvey a moment, will you? Just some questions about equipment on *Bluebelle* need answering."

"Sure," said Captain Barber. "Hold on. I'll get him."

The captain walked into the room where Harvey and Pegg were being interrogated. "They just found a little girl from *Bluebelle*," he said with a wide smile. "She's alive!"

The men in the room stood up, deeply stirred by the news. They turned to look at Harvey. "Oh, my

God!" exclaimed the *Bluebelle's* skipper. Then he added: "Isn't that wonderful?"

"Sure is," agreed Captain Barber. "Mr. Harvey, there's a call for you in the other room."

Harvey left the group as the men talked animatedly about the finding of the little girl. Within a few minutes Harvey re-entered the room. He headed straight for the door.

"Mr. Harvey," a Coast Guard official called to him, "don't you want to ask Mr. Pegg anything about *Bluebelle*? You have a right to."

Harvey shook his head. "No," he replied. "I have to leave."

The others stared after him as he left.

The Sea and Rescue Branch officer's questions to Harvey had been technical and Harvey had answered them easily. He returned to his motel on Miami's Biscayne Boulevard. Slowly, he closed the door behind him. He heard again, in his mind, the words: "They just found a little girl from *Bluebelle*. She's alive."

Harvey made his decision. He walked into the motel room's bathroom and closed the door softly behind him ...

The shadows lengthened in the neat motel room as Florida's sun moved overhead. The room grew dim, then dark, then light again as another day came. At noon a maid arrived to do her daily cleaning. She knocked; there was no answer. She let herself in with her key. Then she froze. A trail of blood oozed from under the bathroom door.

She knocked lightly on the door. She heard nothing. Carefully, she pushed the door open. She screamed, her voice shrill with horror.

The dead eyes of Julian Harvey stared up at her. Sprawled on the tiled floor, the skipper of *Bluebelle* lay bathed in blood. His wrists, legs and throat were slashed. Close to his outstretched fingertips lay a double-edged razor blade.

A suicide note was found with his body. "I got too tired and nervous," it said in part. "I couldn't stand it any longer."

Two pages in length, the note was addressed to his friend James Boozer. It asked him to take care of Harvey's son Lance, 13, who was living in Miami. And it requested burial at sea.

Meanwhile Terry Jo was beginning to talk, eat and smile like any other 11-year-old. But she did not talk about her parents, nor did she mention the tragedy that almost cut short her life.

Her doctor was not worried. "I don't want her to relive what happened until she is ready," he told reporters. "Let her decide for herself. I'll let her take her own good time."

He said that Terry Jo's system was "back to normal" and that she was now sleeping naturally. The guard still stood at her hospital room's door. The Coast Guard remained patient. Terry Jo's availability was up to Dr. Verdon. He waited until November 19th, three days after Terry Jo had been rescued. Then he allowed her to be interviewed. Three Coast Guard investigators entered Terry Jo's room. With them was Dr. Verdon.

They spent an hour in the room, from 3 p.m. to 4 p.m., and when they emerged they were tight-lipped and grim. They said nothing, but the rumour spread that the investigators had heard "quite a story."

Meanwhile the search for Mrs. Harvey and the other members of the Dupperault family continued. A cutter and two aircraft continually criss-crossed a 2,800 square-mile area north-west of Nassau, where *Bluebelle* had vanished.

On November 20th Captain Barber called a news conference in Miami to make Terry Jo's story public. Her account was "lucid and intelligent," he said. "When we went back over it she remained lucid and told the same story with no conflicts. The girl's story is believable. It was told in a straightforward manner. Terry Jo seemed to be in good condition and fairly good spirits throughout the questioning. I think her story is the true one."

It began on the cool evening of that fatal November 12th. *Bluebelle's* sails filled in a soft wind and the ketch proceeded through the Northwest Providence Channel.

The Dupperault family had gathered in the vessel's after cockpit and sat enchanted by the magic of the tropical night. They watched in silence as the sun dipped below the horizon, wallowing in crimson glory.

Terry Jo yawned. Renee also felt sleepy. The two girls waved drowsy "good nights" to their parents and their brother Brian and went to bed. Terry went to her bunk in the ketch's after stateroom. Renee went to hers in the main cabin amidships.

In the descending darkness, *Bluebelle* moved swiftly to her destiny. Terry Jo slept and the night progressed. Then, as if in a mist, her sleep became vaguely troubled; odd noises seemed to invade her slumber; voices and heavy footsteps. Suddenly she was wide awake. Someone was screaming. Feet were running or stamping somewhere on the boat. She listened hard. The screams were coming from her brother Brian!

Terry Jo scrambled out of her bunk and ran for the companionway immediately outside the door to her room. As she was about to mount the stairs she glanced into the central cabin on the starboard side of the companionway. She froze.

Her mother and brother lay on the cabin floor in a pool of blood.

Seeking help, Terry Jo dashed up the companionway to the *Bluebelle's* deck. She looked about her fearfully. Where was everybody? The deck was deserted, eerie in the darkness. No one was steering and the vessel's wheel swung back and forth. More blood glistened on the deck. Then she saw Julian Harvey striding towards her from the forward end, carrying what appeared to be a bucket.

As the tall man loomed over her she cried: "What happened?"

Harvey struck her. "Get below!" he ordered, forcing her to return below decks.

Terry Jo fled to her room and huddled in terror in her bunk. She heard water sloshing somewhere and wondered if Harvey was washing away the blood she had seen on the deck. Then she saw water creeping into her room. She shrank in fear as Harvey suddenly appeared, holding a gun. Terry Jo recalled that a rifle and a pistol were kept somewhere on the boat.

For a moment, Harvey stared at her. Then he turned and left, saying nothing. She heard a strange bumping and hammering sound coming from the deck. The water in her room now covered the floor and was rising rapidly. Terry Jo waited until it reached her bunk and began to lap at her mattress. Then, gathering her courage, she climbed out of the bunk and went up the companionway to the deck.

The first thing she noticed was the *Bluebelle's* dinghy in the water alongside the ketch. A rubber life raft was also in the sea nearby. Harvey appeared again.

"Is the boat sinking?" Terry Jo asked.

"Yes," he replied tersely.

Harvey, she said, then went forward again for a few seconds. He returned and asked Terry Jo if the dinghy had broken loose. She looked and saw the dinghy floating away from the ketch.

Harvey poised for an instant on the deck, then dived into the sea and swam to the dinghy. Terry Jo watched him climb in and float away out of sight in the darkness.

She was alone on a sinking ship's deck. The ketch was rapidly settling in the water. Terry Jo knew that she had just one chance of escaping. She ran to a white cork raft lashed to the top of the main cabin. She tugged furiously at the knots. By the time she had loosened them, the deck was awash. Terry Jo climbed onto the raft and floated away from the sinking ketch.

Then began her astonishing ordeal under blazing tropical sunshine, and black moonless skies.Her raft carried no food or water. The seas that tossed it varied in depth from 60 to 1,000 feet and more. With its white paint, the raft looked like one more white-capped wave among a million others.

During her first night adrift, Terry Jo floated through the Northwest Providence Channel, a predominantly shallow area where waters whip up angrily even under moderate winds. Waves up to eight feet high tossed Terry Jo's precarious craft about crazily, sweeping it to the north. Then as Monday, November 13th, dawned the sun climbed high and soon the temperature reached 85 degrees on the shadeless sea.

Doctors, weathermen and fishermen familiar with Bahamas waters talked later with a reporter from the Fort Lauderdale *News*. They estimated that on her first day at sea Terry Jo was probably not too bothered by the sun. But her thirst rapidly became unbearable. She might have swallowed some sea water, they said, adding to her misery.

On Tuesday, her mouth was horribly dry. She was unable to produce saliva. The sun flared above, beating down without mercy. The sea remained choppy and rough. The constant glare of the sun sent severe pains shooting through her eyes. Leg cramps probably seized her. She could not perspire.

She gazed about her numbly. All she could see was a blue and white wilderness of sea and foam. Sometimes a plane would pass overhead. Terry Jo, trying to shield her eyes from the terrible glare, waved futilely. When darkness fell on Tuesday night, it came as a blessed relief from the heat and the glare.

On Wednesday, if she had slept, Terry Jo awoke delirious. Her pulse rate was increasing rapidly. Dehydration began to affect her body. In all probability, the doctors said, she had suffered a heat stroke that day.

Lack of water caused her circulation rate to slow; less and less blood flowed to her heart. Her body was on fire and cramps gripped her legs. If she had ever felt hungry on the raft, all desire for food had now passed. Without water her digestive juices ceased to function.

During Wednesday, the wind calmed and the seas became placid. But to the 11-year-old girl, now dangerously ill, this had no meaning. She rocked and swayed, alone in a senseless world.

On Thursday, Terry Jo was near to death. Her blood pressure was perilously low; her temperature had probably reached a critical 105 degrees. Her reflexes were gone. She was pitifully sunburned.

But somewhere within her tortured body lay a reserve of strength. When the freighter *Captain Theo* came into her blurred vision, she summoned this last resource.

In her quiet hospital room, Terry Jo rallied. On the day she told the Coast Guard investigators of her nightmare experience on the ketch, her doctor said she had finally relaxed. "Her face became peaceful," he said, "as if a bad dream had been washed away."

Her story directly contradicted Harvey's on several vital points.

She said that at no time did she see, or even smell, fire or smoke. She had seen no broken mast on the deck; but she did say she had seen some bent rail stanchions and that part of the rail's cable had disappeared.

Harvey had been specific in his statement: a sudden squall had snapped his mainmast, sending the broken portion arrow-like through *Bluebelle's* hull. But Terry Jo would only go so far as to say that the mast appeared to be "tipped," or "slanting," but not broken off.

She recalled no arguments involving anyone on the ketch, prior to the catastrophe.

A reporter asked the Coast Guard bluntly: "Are you now prepared to say that Harvey slaughtered everyone aboard *Bluebelle* except Terry Jo, and then left her aboard to die?"

"No comment," was the response.

The *Bluebelle's* owner said: "I think Harvey made up his story. It didn't make sense, for a seaman. I don't know whether he went mad or what. He may have had an accident, but I don't think it happened the way he said."

Julian Harvey's body was taken aboard the luxury yacht *Huckster* in Miami. The dead skipper's friend, James Boozer, appeared thoughtful and sad. The *Huckster* flew the yellow, gold and white pennants — international code for "burial ship." Draped with the American flag, Harvey's coffin stood on the deck.

From a nearby boat, reporters saw a Protestant minister conduct the service. A woman and a teenaged boy stood by. The yacht hove-to and the body slid from beneath the flag and into the water. Boozer tossed an anchor-shaped floral piece after it. An attached blue ribbon read: *"Bon voyage, Julian."*

"Harvey chose this way," Boozer said later, "because he had lost his wife at sea." He remained unconvinced of Harvey's guilt. Virtually alone, he argued that the rescue of Terry Jo had nothing to do with the skipper's suicide.

"I think it was because of his intense love for the girl he married. She was his dream girl. When I met him after he was rescued he was brooding deeply. He told me: 'I don't see why it was Dene instead of me.' He broke down and cried, something I've never seen him do before."

What about Terry Jo's story?

"I don't know," James Boozer said. "There's only one thing that might make me believe it. To slash himself with a razor — well, what must have been his mental condition?"

Boozer tried to collect his dead friend's papers, but the police obtained a court order holding them until the Coast Guard had no further need of them. The papers included bills and letters, indicating that Harvey was in considerable debt. The dead skipper's estate was valued at about $1,500.

Doubts as to whether all the facts in the *Bluebelle* case had come to light were voiced from another quarter. They came from Harvey's brothers-in-law, Charles and Harry Jordan. Both said that they had come to Miami convinced that Harvey had killed their sister Mary Dene and four members of the Dupperault family. "Now," they said, "we're not so sure." Perhaps Harvey told the truth when he said the ketch sank after burning to her waterline, they said. Maybe he panicked in the disaster.

Charles Jordan said that "after talking to people who know about sailing" he had come to believe that Harvey's story was plausible. He thought that perhaps Harvey knew he would be branded a coward for leaving Terry Jo on a sinking ship. This could have caused Harvey to take his own life.

"If he were a homicidal maniac, then why didn't he kill Terry Jo?" Jordan demanded. He added that neither he nor his brother were satisfied that the Coast Guard investigation was complete: they still wanted to ascertain whether or not their sister was dead.

The brothers asked to talk to Terry Jo, but permission was refused. No member of the public was allowed to see the little girl, still in her hospital room.

Then the investigation of *Bluebelle's* end turned to the background of its tall, sun-tanned skipper. If Harvey had perpetrated mass murder aboard the ketch, was it a case of homicidal mania, without rational explanation? Or if Harvey was sane, what was the motive?

Almost immediately, investigators found a possible answer. In September 1961, Harvey had taken out two insurance policies on himself. In the event of accidental death they would have paid $100,000 in benefits.

Then investigators found that, a month earlier, he had taken out a policy on his wife. It had a double-indemnity clause that would pay him $40,000 in the event of her accidental death.

The probe reached back to the strange car accident 12 years before in Florida, when Julian Harvey had emerged alive from the crash that had killed his second wife and her mother.

Steve DeCosta, a skin-diver who recovered the bodies of the two women trapped in the car, recalled: "That car was upside-down in twelve feet of water. I thought it looked suspicious at the time. The door on the driver's side was open. I don't see how a man could have climbed out alive, unless he was prepared, with his hand already on the door handle."

In Dallas, Texas, a woman said that she might be Harvey's third or second wife, she wasn't sure which. She said that when she had read of his suicide she thought that it was due to his bereavement and the loss of the Dupperault family.

"But after I read the little girl's story," she said, "I wasn't so sure." She paused. "My present husband and I have talked this over. We feel I'm lucky to be alive."

She said that Harvey had told her she was his second wife when she married him in 1950. "He told me about Joan, the wife who was killed in the wreck. He said that the car went off the road and that Joan and her mother were killed. But I've been told since that he apparently did not make any effort to rescue them."

She said that she and Harvey were divorced in 1953, after he returned from Korea. "At least," she concluded, "he never insured *me*."

Terry Jo sat cheerfully in her green-walled hospital room, looking like one more doll among the 15 that had arrived since the story of her ordeal was published. Her favourite was "Pattie," sent to her by the crew of *Captain Theo*, her rescuers.

She smiled happily, all trace of her experience gone, except for small patches of sunburn on her cheeks, nose and forehead.

Her aunt visited her often. Letters and cards

arrived by the bundle. "As soon as I get home," she wrote to a friend in Green Bay, "I'll take the kitten you said I could have. I'd like to have it now."

But on Thanksgiving Day her smile faded when she was told that her family had finally been given up for dead.

Coast Guard officers believed Terry Jo's story but felt that it was incomplete. Her interview with the investigators had been tape-recorded, and the transcript showed that she had made only one spontaneous answer of any length. This was when she was asked to tell in her own words how the sinking occurred.

Virtually everything else had been elicited by direct questions from Captain Barber or his assistant, Lieutenant Ernest Murdock; to these she answered simply: "Yes," or "No."

In her unprompted telling of the story she did not account for several members of her family. Nor did she speculate on what might have happened to her mother and brother, who she said she saw lying in a pool of blood.

One of Miami's most highly respected interrogators, Homicide Detective Warren Holmes, a lie-detector expert, said he was convinced that there was more to be learned from Terry Jo. But in Green Bay her teacher said: "I've never known her to lie. If you're asking me if Terry Jo made up her story about the *Bluebelle* sinking, the answer is absolutely 'No.'"

More aspects of the strange case were probed. Some officials were reported to be considering the possibility that Julian Harvey had had an accomplice and that he had planned to meet him — or her — afterwards. Had Harvey never intended to be rescued by a merchant vessel? Had it been his plan instead to rendezvous with another small boat at a prearranged location?

The sunken ketch meanwhile kept her secrets. Her owner said that there was little or no chance of ever learning them. "It is ridiculous even to consider a search in water more than a mile deep.

"If there was the slightest chance, I'd try, just to get answers to some of the questions. But it would be foolish."

The Coast Guard fixed the location of the sinking at about Latitude 25.55 north and Longitude 77.38 west. This put the ketch in the Northwest Providence Channel, which in some places is several miles deep. Professional salvage men and oceanographic scientists agreed that even if the wreck were found — which was unlikely — divers would be unable to reach it.

Then James Boozer, Harvey's old and trusting friend, re-entered the case. Mystified Coast Guard officers were asked to come to the office of Dr. John Hanger, pastor of the First Methodist Church of Coral Gables, Florida. Mr. Boozer was there with Dr. Hanger.

He revealed a story which, he said, Harvey had made him take a vow never to tell. He said that, after a conference with his minister, Dr. Hanger, he had decided to break his promise.

"It was after Harvey had been rescued and before Terry Jo was found," James Boozer said. "Harvey came to me in an extremely nervous state. I reminded him that most of the other bodies from the *Bluebelle* would drift ashore and be picked up somehow. I said I hoped his story would match with those of any survivors who might be found.

"At this point I asked him point blank: 'Harvey, why don't you tell me what really happened out there?' Before I could get the words out of my mouth he stood up quickly. Looking me straight in the eye, he said: 'Will you take a vow on Lance (Harvey's 13-year-old son) that you will never repeat what I am going to tell you?' I promised him, and he told me the story about the squall coming up, saying that his wife and Mr. Dupperault were knocked into the sea by the falling mast.

"Then he said, 'I lost my nerve when I saw the blood on the deck and I jumped overboard. The next thing I knew I was pulling the little girl (Renee) into a boat with me.' "

Boozer said that he felt certain that Harvey had told him the truth. He said that he was equally sure that Harvey had intended to commit suicide "long before it was announced that Terry Jo had been found."

The Coast Guard officers left, their faces expressionless. The story contrasted oddly with Harvey's past as an iron-nerved pilot and daring yachtsman.

On November 26th the Coast Guard decided to question Terry Jo again. They emerged from her hospital room more convinced than ever that she had told the truth. "We asked her the questions in the roughest sort of way," a Coast Guard spokesman said. "We planned the questions with the idea of trying to trip her up. But she told a straightforward story and did not deviate from it. This child could not possibly be evading anything."

Harry Jordan, brother of Harvey's wife Mary Dene, reached a similar conclusion. "I am convinced," he said, "after talking to everyone concerned, that Harvey originally intended to kill only my sister."

He drew attention to the $20,000 double-indemnity insurance policy on Mary Dene which Harvey had taken out only during September. "He apparently wanted the $40,000 he would collect for her 'accidental death' to buy a new boat." Jordan added that Harvey had probably been surprised by Arthur Dupperault in the act of killing his wife and had then decided to kill everyone else on board to cover up the crime.

On November 27th Terry Jo, now once again a vivacious 11-year-old, returned with relatives to her aunt's home in Green Bay.

Many questions remained unresolved. Why had Harvey spared her? Had his conscience stayed his hand? Did he consider leaving Terry Jo to drown — instead of being butchered or thrown overboard — a mitigation of his crime? If so, why did he leave Terry Jo alive with another life-raft on board? Or did he dismiss the possibility that she would think of the raft and succeed in launching it?

Did he pick up Renee's body to give added credence to his tale of disaster when he was rescued or reached shore? But how could he know either would occur? Weather is fickle in Bahamas waters. Did he, wise in the ways of that sea, really get into an open boat without compass or provisions? Or was the dinghy supplied with these? Were they hastily thrown overboard when Harvey sighted his approaching rescuer, the tanker *Gulflion*?

If he intended to rendezvous with an accomplice, was someone living in dread of discovery, of a knock on the door? Or did something happen aboard *Bluebelle* that Terry Jo, in her childish innocence, was unable to comprehend?

Only one thing was certain. Although Terry Jo's prediction had come tragically true for the rest of her family, she at least was now safe.

The ketch Bluebelle

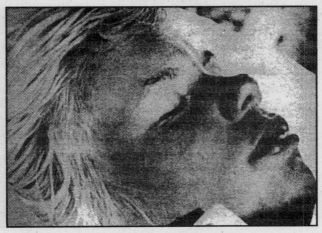

Terry Jo Dupperault.
A little girl's bad dream? Or did it really happen?

Terry Jo in hospital.
Right, the Bluebelle's
skipper, Julian Harvey

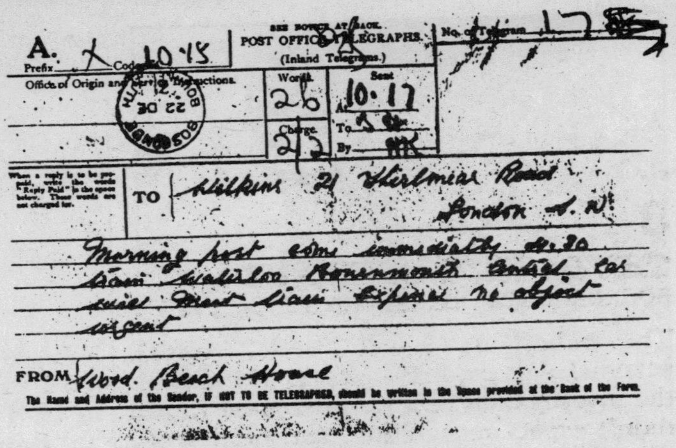
SEE NOTICE AT BACK.
POST OFFICE TELEGRAPHS.
(Inland Telegrams.)
No. of Telegram 17
A. Prefix X Code 10.15
Office of Origin and Service Instructions.
BOSCOMBE 22 DE 12
Words 26
Charge 2/2
Sent 10.17
When a reply is to be prepaid, write the words "Reply Paid" in the space below. These words are not charged for.
TO Wilkins 21 Wirlmere Road London S.W.
Morning post come immediately 11.30 train Waterloo Bournemouth Central car meet train expense no object urgent
FROM Wood. Beech House
The Name and Address of the Sender, IF NOT TO BE TELEGRAPHED, should be written in the Space provided at the Back of the Form.

The fatal telegram: see opposite

8
THE SPIRIT OF IRENE
BOURNEMOUTH, DECEMBER 22ND, 1921

The police are usually understandably loth to acknowledge psychic help. Spiritualists involved in the investigation of a Bournemouth murder in 1921 didn't expect recognition, and none was given. But the spirit world nevertheless played a part behind the scene ...

The saga began five days before Christmas when a 31-year-old woman sent an advertisement to the *Morning Post*. The ad. read: *Lady cook, 31, requires post in school. Experienced in school with 40 boarders. Disengaged. Salary £65. Miss Irene Wilkins, 21 Thirlmere Road, Streatham, S.W.16.*

The details appeared in the *Morning Post* of December 22nd. Before midday a telegraph boy was knocking at Irene Wilkins's front door. A few seconds later she called out to her mother and sister.

"Look!" she said excitedly, waving the telegram. "It's a reply to my advert in today's *Morning Post*. They want me at once. Isn't it wonderful? Just like a Christmas present!"

Her mother was delighted. It seemed that Irene's luck had changed at last. Of course, she would be missed at home, but jobs were scarce in the post-war slump of 1921; and Irene had found it hard to settle down in civilian life after serving during the war in the Women's Army Auxiliary Corps.

Her mother read the telegram a second time:

Morning Post. Come immediately 4.30 train Waterloo Bournemouth Central. Car will meet train. Expense no object Urgent. Wood, Beech House.

It did not occur to the widow and her daughter to wonder what could be urgent about installing a cook in a school whose pupils had presumably gone home for the Christmas holidays.

And had Irene seen the original scrawl of the telegram handed in at Bournemouth she would have been suspicious. For in that filed slip of paper, "expense" was misspelled with a "c" and Bournemouth had no central "e."

Shortly after the telegram arrived Irene Wilkins went out to wire a reply. This stated simply that she was catching the 4.30 train to Bournemouth. Just as it was steaming out of Waterloo Station another Post Office messenger arrived at 21 Thirlmere Road. He presented an astonished Mrs. Wilkins with an envelope containing the draft telegram her daughter had sent to "Wood, Beach House, Bournemouth." It was accompanied by a Post Office note saying that the telegram was being returned to the sender because both address and addressee were unknown, so delivery was impossible.

"What can it mean?" Mrs. Wilkins asked her other daughter anxiously. "There must be some mistake."

On the same 4.30 train from Waterloo to Bournemouth was Frank Humphries. He was a middle-aged consulting engineer and designer who lived in Boscombe, a Bournemouth suburb, and he had arranged for a car to meet the train at Bournemouth Central. On alighting, however, he found that the car had not arrived. Turning towards the station exit, he noticed a young woman walking just ahead of him.

Tall and slim, she wore a chocolate-coloured suede hat with a red insertion round the crown that ended in an untied bow on the left side — a very chic piece of millinery that winter. She was wearing a brown coat of a darker shade than her hat, he noticed, and in one hand she carried an attaché-case. But it was the colourful and snappy little hat that caught his eye.

He saw it again, a few minutes later, after once more looking for the car that had failed to arrive for him. The woman was sitting beside a man wearing a chauffeur's peaked cap. Humphries watched her being borne away in a greenish-grey car, one of several parked by the station entrance. The chauffeur turned the car, and the brown hat with the untied scarlet knot vanished into the December dusk.

Frank Humphries promptly forgot about the saucy little hat — but he was reminded of it again forcibly on January 4th, when he again saw the greenish-grey car. By then, too, the hat was familiar to most newspaper readers in Britain.

It was shortly after daybreak on December 23rd when a labourer named Nicklen walked to work down the Iford-Tuckton lane, between Bournemouth and Christchurch. On the far side of a strung-wire fence he saw three cows nosing a dark object that lay in the field. Thinking that the cows were behaving curiously, he climbed the fence and approached them. He then saw that the object that had attracted the cows was the sprawled body of a young woman whose clothes had been dragged high around her waist.

With a hand that shook badly, the labourer stooped and touched the blood-smeared face. It was icy cold. He turned and ran to report the discovery.

By nine o'clock that morning a police surgeon confirmed that the woman had been murdered.

Her dark-brown coat was soaked with melting frost. Her chocolate-brown hat with scarlet insertion was found in a gorse bush. Frost and mud had removed the saucy touch that had caught Frank Humphries's eye at Bournemouth Central only a few hours earlier. The wearer had died of haemorrhage and shock resulting from savage wounds to the head and brain.

The spot where Irene Wilkins's body was found lay to the east of Bournemouth, in an area about to be taken over for speculative building. New roads had already been laid across fields, and housing estates planned. One of the new thoroughfares was called Seafield Road. It ran from the Iford-Tuckton lane, providing a way through for the car carrying Inspector Brewer and Sergeant Fisher of the local police, who arrived by 8.20 a.m. They found PC Chiverton guarding the remains of Irene Wilkins. And when Dr. Simmons arrived half an hour after Inspector Brewer, it was to find the officer examining a woman's umbrella.

"It was leaning against the wire fence, and there's blood on the handle," said the inspector.

Ten minutes later the doctor rose from examining the corpse. He rubbed his hands to restore feeling to his fingers numbed by the cold.

"It was a man, Inspector, but he didn't get what he was trying for. Her hips and thighs and the lower parts of her arms are badly bruised. She was only about five-foot-four, but she put up a damned good fight, whoever she was."

No money or personal papers were found with the body. News of the murder was released to the Press, together with the victim's description, and it wasn't long before the police at Streatham were telephoning the name of the murdered woman to their colleagues in Bournemouth.

By Christmas Eve a full-scale manhunt was launched, led by Superintendent Garrett who set great store by the decoy telegram he had traced to a particular post-office. He was also interested in some Dunlop Magnum tyre-prints found by Inspector Brewer in Seafield Road. The vehicle which had left the impressions had apparently parked at a point opposite the field.

The weather on the night of the murder proved to be of some help to the police. Until about 8 p.m. there had been a sequence of chilling drizzles. Then the sky had cleared, with a cold wind drying the ground. The mud on the victim's hat and the damp state of her clothes suggested that, at latest, the crime was committed by 8.20. It was established that she had been dragged through the wire fence which was about three feet high. That probably meant that she was insensible from the heavy blows on the head or already dead. Bruising on the lower part of her face pointed to a fist having felled her. The injuries to her head could have been caused by a hammer.

The picture was becoming clearer with each hour that passed, but there was a startling development after Garrett traced the origin of the decoy telegram. His checking had turned up a similar cable, sent from Bournemouth on December 20th, offering a post to a woman and suggesting that an urgent appointment be kept.

"Keep watching," Garrett told his men at the local Post Offices. "Keep searching."

Sure enough they turned up a third decoy telegram. This one had not been sent from Bournemouth, but from Boscombe on December 17th.

When the recipients of the first two decoy telegrams were traced, one said she had simply changed her mind about going to Bournemouth. The other had packed her bag and made the journey, but had not been met as arranged. Annoyed, she had tried to find the address given on the telegram, but there was no such address in the town.

The police were anxious to trace a man of no great literacy who drove a vehicle with Dunlop Magnum tyres. Garrett believed that such a car had been at Bournemouth Central to meet the train on which Irene Wilkins travelled from Waterloo. There was little margin of time between the train's arrival and the murder. It seemed that Irene Wilkins was met as promised in the decoy telegram, and then driven straight to her death. It also seemed reasonable to believe that the car and its driver were still in the Bournemouth area.

Garrett instigated a check of cars in the district, especially those fitted with Dunlop Magnum tyres. Dozens of chauffeurs were interviewed and asked to provide alibis for the evening of December 22nd. Passengers who had used Bournemouth Central at the time of the arrival of the 4.30 train from Waterloo were also interviewed. One of the most interesting statements was made by Frank Humphries.

He not only witnessed Irene Wilkins sitting next to a man in a chauffeur's uniform at the wheel of a greenish-grey touring car on that day. On January 4th he saw both car and chauffeur again, and took particular note of the driver's appearance and the car's registration number — LK 7405.

On the second occasion Humphries was queuing at the ticket window. He was sure that the car had the same chauffeur at the wheel and he called to his son: "Get the number of that car — quick!"

His son scribbled the number on a box of matches. Garrett learned that LK 7405 was the number of a green-grey Mercedes owned by a Mr. Sutton of Barton Close, Southbourne. The police file of car-drivers' statements included one made by Thomas Henry Allaway, a chauffeur employed by Sutton. Garrett noticed that his alibi for the approximate time of the murder, between 7.30 and 8.15, depended entirely on the man's unsupported word.

Inquiries were made about the 36-year-old chauffeur. He was a Londoner, born in Kilburn, married, and had a seven-year-old daughter. Mrs. Allaway was living with her parents in Reading, where her husband was also well known. His employer and his employer's wife gave him a good reference, but his Army record was bad. It showed a spell in a military prison for desertion from the Royal Army Service Corps in 1916 while on leave from France.

Garrett held a conference and issued instructions. "I want an identity parade," he announced. "And I want each Post Office girl who took those decoy telegrams to attend."

While the investigation progressed, Irene Wilkins's attaché-case was found in thick shrubbery at Branksome Park, eight miles from Seafield Road. That might have held little interest for Garrett, save for a significant detail already on record. Mrs. Sutton's sister resided in Branksome Park and Allaway had driven her there on December 23rd.

The police also traced a newsagent named Samways, who remembered a chauffeur buying a *Morning Post* from him at about 10 o'clock on the morning of December 22nd.

"What makes you recall the chauffeur?" Samways was asked.

"Well, that's easy," said the shopkeeper. "Mr. Da Costa was in here at the time. You'd better ask him. He'll tell you."

Both Da Costa and Samways gave descriptions of the chauffeur, who had told them that he expected to pick a winner that day. But he did not turn to the sporting page when he opened his newspaper. The descriptions given of the chauffeur fitted Allaway.

Garrett was on the point of pulling his man in, but Allaway moved first. When the police called at his address they found his wife in tears. The little flat in Windsor Road, Boscombe, was filled with furniture the Allaways had previously kept stored in Barker's depository in Kensington. Mrs. Allaway had at last been about to enjoy a real home of her own.

"Like a dream come true," she had told a friend only days before. "After being so long on the move."

But it was a dream that was to become a nightmare, like much of her life with her husband. Allaway was morose and dour, a man of strange silences that at times exploded in anger, often accompanied by cruelty.

"Has your husband much cash, Mrs. Allaway?" Garrett asked the abandoned wife.

"He's broke," she replied. "He's been losing heavily on the horses."

But the wanted man, Garrett soon learned, had stolen a cheque-book from his employer, who reported that there were about a dozen blank cheques in the book at the time of the theft.

Mrs. Allaway, and her daughter left Boscombe to return to Reading. Soon afterwards the police again heard from Mr. Sutton. The missing cheque-book was being put to good use by the fugitive. He had talked local tradespeople into cashing three forged cheques. Because they were for small sums, and because he was known as Mr. Sutton's chauffeur, the shopkeepers had readily obliged. A total of about £20 was involved.

Inspector Brewer was dispatched to Kilburn, where he picked up news of Allaway, now calling himself Cook, but he just missed his man. He telephoned Garrett, who lost no time in contacting the Reading police. They sent a detective to watch the home of Mrs. Allaway's parents.

Allaway eventually appeared at the end of the street. He seemed nervous, constantly glancing over his shoulder. He halted when he saw the plainclothes officer, stared across the street at him, then turned about and walked away quickly. He broke into a run. The officer hurried after him, calling on him to stop. A passer-by stuck out a foot, and Allaway tripped and went sprawling. Before he could rise the detective was standing over him.

Tom Allaway spent that night in a police cell. Next morning he was returned to Bournemouth where he was charged with stealing the cheque-book from his employer and with issuing forged cheques in Boscombe. The magistrate remanded him to Winchester prison.

An identification parade was arranged. The three girl Post Office clerks were asked to attend to identify the man who handed in the decoy telegrams. A dozen men appeared in the line-up, and Emmeline Barnes, who accepted the telegram for Irene Wilkins, failed to make a positive identification.

Lilian Diplock, who handled the first decoy telegram, first identified a man who was not Allaway but who looked like him. She was given a second try, and this time she picked out the suspect and was positive about her selection.

Then it was the turn of Alice Waters who had accepted the second of the three telegrams. She told Garrett that when she first read through the draft she had to query a word with the sender.

"It looked as though he had written 'ear will meet,' so I asked him what the word was," she explained. "He said it was 'car.' He repeated the word car. I remember, too, that he spoke in a sort of husky voice."

"As though he had a cold, Miss Waters?"

"No, it was a natural huskiness, I should say."

At the identity parade she singled out Allaway without hesitation. Garrett then decided to try another test. He had the girl turn her back. Allaway was taken out of the line and put in another position. Then each of the men in the parade was asked to say, "car — car will meet," repeating the words Alice Waters remembered. When it was Allaway's turn, Miss Waters said instantly: "That's the man."

Garrett asked him if he would make a written statement. The prisoner hesitated, then agreed. He was provided with stationery and began writing in a severely upright hand, very different from the sloping scrawl of the decoy telegrams. Before he was halfway through the statement, however, his handwriting changed several times, gradually beginning to resemble that telltale scrawl. The statement also had its quota of misspellings:

"I Thomas Henry Allaway, beg to state that I am innocent of the crime brought against me. On the night of 22nd December, 1921, I left my master's house, no. 8 Clifton Road, Southbourne, about 5.30 p.m., proceeding to my garage in Haviland Road, Boscombe, by way of Southbourne Grove. On my way I met and picked up the cook from the house and gave her a lift as far as Ashley Road corner, leaving her there. I proceeded to my garage, arriving about 5.45 p.m. After putting the car away, Mr. Barrett passed a remark about had I finished. I said yes and went home to my tea. That was the last time I saw the car that evening.

"After having my tea, my wife said she would like to go to the pictures, which she usually done every Monday and Thursday. I left my lodgins with my wife and child about 6.45 p.m. and leaving her at the Working Mans Club I promiss to meet her at 8.45 at the Salisbury Hotel.

"Whilst I was in the club I met Mr. Barrett and he ask me why I hadn't gone to the pictures, and I told him that I did not care about them. We stood talking at the bar until he was ready to start a game of Billiards with a friend, name Mr. Nicholls, that would be about 7.15.

"I went and sat down to watch the play for a little while. I then went out to get an *Evening News* from a boy who stands at the corner of Ashley Road and Haviland Road. I remember the time quite well as I have to wait a few minutes before the paper came up about 7.20 to 7.30 p.m.

"After getting the *Evening News* I went back to my lodgins and sat by the fire reading until about 8 o'clock, and before going out I asked my landlord if he would like to look at the *Evening News*, and I Borowed his *Echo*. I went back to my room. I did not find much to read in the *Echo* so I made the fire up and went back to the Club, which would be about 8.15 p.m. Whilst in the club I remember seeing a Mr. Patrick playing a game of Snooker on no. 5 table. I nodded to him but he did not speak. I finished up my drink and left the club and took a gentle walk towards the Salisbury Hotel, arriving there about 8.30 p.m.

"In the Salisbury I meet several people I knew and who I can call to prove I was there. My wife came in a little late, about 8.55, and we stopped there until 10 o'clock, after that we went home and was in bed by 10.30 the latest.

"T. H. Allaway."

In short, on the night of the murder he had not been in the Mercedes at Bournemouth Central, and he had not driven the car to Seafield Road. He also denied having sent the decoy telegram to Streatham.

Witnesses who had seen Allaway on the night of the murder gave differing times. These did not add up to a watertight alibi.

Mrs. Sutton disproved one of the chauffeur's claims. He had stated that he could not have handed the third decoy telegram to Emmeline Barnes at the time logged on it — 10.17 a.m. — because he was on duty, and had been since 10 o'clock, yet Mrs. Sutton said that Allaway's duties during December and January commenced at 10.30. He would thus have had ample time to send the telegram to Streatham.

On the morning of Christmas Eve, Allaway had been seen in Portman Mews where the Mercedes was garaged, changing one of the rear tyres, which were both Dunlop Magnums. He replaced the tyre with a Michelin. That morning newspapers had carried the story of the Magnum treads discovered at Seafield Road by Inspector Brewer.

Garrett also learned why the girl who received another of the decoy telegrams was not met by the sender. Mr. Sutton was unexpectedly employing both car and chauffeur at the time of her arrival.

Thomas Henry Allaway's trial opened on July 3rd, 1922, before Mr. Justice Avory at Winchester Assizes. It lasted four days, and the defendant elected to go into the witness-box. This brought him under fierce cross-examination from the prosecution and he proved a most unreliable witness for the defence. He was shifty, hesitant and obviously unsure of where he was allowing his evidence to take him.

He insisted that he had not written certain items produced by the prosecution. These were letters and postcards sent to his wife at various intervals before the murder. He maintained that they had been written by someone else. The prosecution called a handwriting expert, Mr. Gurrin, to give evidence. He refuted all Allaway's claims, including one about a friend writing at his dictation, the chauffeur having hurt his hand when cranking a car-engine.

The trial was notable for an odd incident. The background to this was that early in the investigation a Boscombe woman medium had felt sure that the killer of Irene Wilkins was still in the area. Together with friends, she visited the crime scene and she became convinced of her ability to help the investigators. She wrote to the police suggesting that efforts should be made to contact the victim's spirit. Predictably, she received no reply.

Then an officer happened to call at the medium's home about a trivial, unrelated matter. He was so impressed by what she told him that he reported the conversation to his superiors. A number of séances followed at which Bournemouth police officers were present, bringing with them some of Irene Wilkins's clothing. Through the medium, the victim's spirit described the killer and subsequent séances identified his home. The role of the occult in the investigation was later chronicled by one of the participants in a small volume, *The Spirit of Irene*.

At Allaway's trial a material date was disputed. It was important that this should be established by one of the prosecution's witnesses, and he had forgotten it. He was one of those who had taken part in the séances and he now hesitated for some moments in the witness box.

"My mind," he said afterwards, "was a perfect blank. Then I remembered that 'Pat' had promised to help us, and mentally I asked him to do so."

'Pat' was one of the spirits invoked at the séances.

"Immediately," the witness continued, "it was as if a sheet of paper was placed before my eyes on which was written in large letters 'January 6th.'"

It proved to be the correct date.

Mr. Justice Avory, in his summing-up, went out of his way to acknowledge the value of Mr. Gurrin's evidence relating to the handwriting on the originals of the decoy telegrams. But he told the jury:

"You are not bound by his conclusions and it is for you to say whether you come to the same conclusions — namely, that these telegrams were written by the same person, and that person is the prisoner."

The jury were absent for an hour, and their verdict was one of guilty. Allaway gasped. His dark face turned purple as he groaned: "I am innocent of this crime absolutely."

A month later his appeal was dismissed, but Allaway maintained his shifty tactics until the morning of his execution by John Ellis. In the early hours of August 19th, 1922, his wife and brother visited him and he solemnly told them that he was innocent. Yet he had admitted his guilt to the prison governor only the previous evening.

But what was his murder motive? None was ever established and why lure a woman from London when with a Mercedes he could have simply picked up a local woman?

Thomas Allaway in the dock during his trial for murder. Below, his victim dumped in a field and X shows where he parked his car

9

SOMETIMES HE WAS FIGHTING WITH DOGS AND HORSES
GLASGOW, APRIL 10TH, 1878

Never mind high technology's "virtual reality." In Scotland, Simon Fraser had his own virtual reality more than a century ago. No hi-tech equipment was needed to create his large-as-life illusions, and to Simon they were so real that he'd kill for them.

By day the 27-year-old Scot worked at a sawmill. At night he returned to his wife and 18-month-old son at the family's small terraced house in Lime Street, Glasgow. And it was always at night that Simon's trouble began.

Nightmares were his problem: dreams so vivid that to Simon they were for real. Wild animals took shape, intent on killing him. He couldn't just lie there to be savaged. He had to act swiftly to defend himself. He had to destroy them.

The horrors that arose in his dreams had plagued him from childhood. His stepmother had put tubs of water on the floor beside his bed to wake him when he stepped out in his sleep, but this didn't always work. Sometimes he jumped straight out of bed, clearing the tubs in his haste to repel whatever was threatening him.

Relatives were well aware that while slumbering the

normally kindly Simon could become a man of violence. Some of them had been on the receiving end, but it wasn't something they talked about. It was a family matter, a personal problem the Frasers kept to themselves. Until one day in 1878, when it could be concealed no longer ...

The one thing upon which everyone agreed was that Simon Fraser doted on his son. He couldn't do too much for him, loved showing him off to friends and relations, and generally made such a fuss of him that Simon's wife feared he was spoiling the child.

But in the early hours of April 10th this picture of domestic bliss was shattered. At 1 a.m. Mrs. Janet McEwen, who lived nearby, was wakened by someone knocking at her door with an urgency that wouldn't take snores for an answer. On her doorstep was Simon Fraser.

"He was wringing his hands and seemed in great distress," she said later. "He asked me to go and see his bairn. I went to his house and saw his wife, who was screaming. The child was unconscious on her knee.

"Mr. Fraser was terribly excited and kept calling the child 'my dear' and 'my dear little son.' He wasn't pretending. He seemed quite sincere in his distress. I asked him who had done this awful thing, and he said: 'It was me that did it, mistress. I did it through my sleep.'"

The child died at 3 a.m. Later Simon Fraser was to tell the police and a doctor how he had picked up his slumbering son and battered his head against a wall. But he hadn't known he was doing it. "You see, I was fast asleep at the time," he said.

The explanation was repeated at the High Court of the Justiciary in Edinburgh on July 15th. But would the judge or jury accept it? From the sentences Lord

Moncrieff, the Lord Justice-Clerk, had been handing out, things didn't look good for Simon Fraser. Two men had each received seven years' penal servitude for trivial thefts. Following that, only one penalty seemed possible for child-murder.

The charge spelt out the crime in grim detail. It alleged that Simon Fraser "did wickedly and feloniously attack Simon Fraser junior, a child of eighteen months, did seize him violently and did throw or push him several times against the door or walls of the house, and thereby did fracture his skull and lacerate his brain so that he was mortally injured and was thus murdered."

"I am not guilty," Fraser responded. "I am guilty in my sleep but not in my senses."

Mrs. McEwen told the court that she had asked him if he habitually walked in his sleep. "He said he used to do it when he was a boy. Then he told me he thought he'd seen a beast running through the room. It leaped into the bed and he seized hold of it."

The court heard next from Dr. Alexander Jamieson, who had been called to the house by Fraser. "He told me he thought he had killed his child," said the physician. "I found the child Simon in convulsions, and he was dying. There was a severe injury on his forehead, such as would be caused by the head being driven against the wall or floor.

"Fraser told me that in his nightmare he thought the baby was a wild beast. He also said he had been violent before whilst sleep-walking — that he had used violence against his half-sister and his wife."

The child had died at 3 a.m., and in his distress Simon Fraser had run from his house to the Rutherglen Road home of John Pritchard, a fellow-worker at the sawmill. "Wee Simon is dead, and it is me that is the cause of it," Fraser had told his friend.

Asked in the witness-box what sort of father Fraser had been, Pritchard replied, "I can answer you that question without any doubt. We used to go visiting at his house quite a lot and I could see he was very fond of his child — none more so."

Confirming this opinion, Fraser's father told the court that his son was, however, less than bright. "Ever since he was little there was a dullness and stupidity about him. He could not learn his lessons at school. It was a common thing for him to rise during the night and go through capers."

"These capers — what form did they take?" asked the Public Prosecutor.

"All sorts, really. Sometimes he supposed the house was on fire, and sometimes he was fighting with dogs and horses. They weren't there, if you follow me, but he was fighting with them. His eyes would be open, but I knew he wasn't awake. He spoke, but what he said was nonsense."

Fraser's father went on to tell how at 14 his son had dreamt that a white stallion, jaws foaming, eyes glowing green, was stampeding through the house, crushing the family and smashing the furniture. Simon had leapt from his bed to attack the animal ... and his father had woken to find the boy on top of him, pummelling and clawing at his face.

When the family were living in Norway, the father continued, Simon had wandered out of the house and into the sea in his sleep. He had apparently been having a nightmare in which his half-sister Elspeth was drowning, and he had gone to save her. This contrasted with the time she awoke to find him attempting to strangle her, under the impression that she was a ferocious beast. He had also once pulled his wife out of bed by her legs in the middle of the night, believing he was rescuing her from a fire.

He had only once injured himself sleepwalking — and then he had been so deeply immersed in his dream that the pain from the toe he had broken didn't wake him.

Simon Fraser's mother-in-law bitterly blamed him for the death of her cherished grandson, but even she had to admit that Simon simply didn't know what he was doing when his nightmares beset him. One night at the Frasers' home had been enough for her. Her son-in-law had started shrieking as he battled with a mad dog in his dream. She was so frightened, she told the court, that the next day she had gone home to Dundee.

"Do you consider him to be a stupid man?" asked the prosecutor.

"Perhaps it was his want of education that made him seem a little droll," the mother-in-law replied, as if trying to fathom what had attracted her daughter to Simon Fraser.

By now the jury felt they had heard enough. Their foreman rose to tell the judge that they could see little point in hearing further evidence: all were agreed that Fraser had not been responsible for his actions.

That concurred with his own view, Lord Moncrieff told the jurors. Nevertheless, he felt they should hear medical evidence concerning the prisoner.

Realising there would be no murder conviction, the prosecutor switched to another objective. This was to have Simon Fraser locked up as a lunatic, so that he was no longer a danger to others.

If a man's nightmares triggered violence, should he be confined in an asylum? That was what the court now had to decide.

Dr. Yellowlees, superintendent of a local mental institution, was the prosecution's first expert witness. He told the court: "Somnambulism is a state of unhealthy brain activity, coming on during sleep, of very varying intensity — sometimes little more than restless sleep, sometimes developing into delusions and violence amounting really to insanity. This man labours under somnambulism in its most aggravated form."

The prosecutor asked the doctor if he attributed Simon Fraser's condition to a mental disorder.

"To the abnormal condition of the brain," Dr. Yellowlees replied. "That is the case in every instance of delusion, even when there is no insanity."

The prosecutor pressed the physician further. When Fraser was in a somnambulistic state, he asked, was he in effect insane?

"The word 'insane' describes his condition or nature," the doctor replied obligingly.

But Mr. C. S. Dickson, defending, won from Dr. Yellowlees the admission that he had found Fraser to be "below average intelligence ... but practically sane when I examined him."

And just how expert was this expert witness? Was he an authority on somnambulism, asked Mr. Dickson.

The doctor made no reply. The question was asked again. Reluctantly, Dr. Yellowlees confessed, "I have no experience of somnambulism. That is to say, I have not seen a man in his condition."

Then the prosecution called Dr. Alex Robertson, medical officer and surgeon at Glasgow's City Parochial Asylum and City Poorhouse. "I have had considerable experience of abnormal conditions of the brain. I know the facts of this case and I am of the opinion that the prisoner was insane when he committed this act," Robertson said bluntly.

"A dreamer fancies he sees and feels objects, but this man really did see and feel," the doctor went on.

"He saw and felt a child in reality and mistook it for a beast."

Dr. Robertson said he believed Fraser's somnambulism "was just short fits of insanity that came on during sleep. In medical parlance there is no name for this particular kind of delusion. It is altogether exceptional."

Dr. Clouston, of Morningside, Edinburgh, was the only medical witness called by the defence. In contrast to the self-assured Robertson, he seemed diffident to the point of nervousness. But he had interviewed Simon Fraser, and the prisoner had clearly impressed him as a basically sensible, caring man. Fraser had seemed to have "fair judgment for his education" and to have a particularly affectionate nature.

"I asked him if he felt very much over the death of his child," Dr. Clouston told the court. "He said that he had, but as his wife had felt it so much more, he had concealed his own feelings and appeared calm for her sake."

Pointing out that Fraser's case was not unique, the doctor recalled a church missionary in Yorkshire, an eminently respectable man who had been so impressed by the figure of a murder victim in a waxworks display that the spectacle still haunted him when he went to bed early after visiting the exhibition.

"His wife came into the room about an hour afterwards and he started up, thinking she was a robber coming to rob his house. He would have throttled her if a neighbour had not come to the rescue."

The medical profession had not as yet defined any act which occurred during sleep as insanity, Dr. Clouston concluded, in response to cross-examination by the prosecution. "There is merely an abnormal condition of the brain producing delusion and violence."

Wasn't that the same thing as insanity? asked the prosecutor.

"We do not regard it as such," Dr. Clouston replied. "A sane man may have delusions during sleep which, while sleep lasts, he believes are true. In that state he is not morally responsible when that develops into action because he is not conscious of the true nature of what he is doing."

The judge now addressed the jury. There appeared to be not the slightest doubt, he told them, that Fraser had been totally unconscious of his act. Labouring under a delusion while in a state of somnambulism, he had acted under the belief that he was trying to kill a beast.

"It is a matter of some consequence to the prisoner whether he is considered to be insane or simply as not responsible," Lord Moncrieff continued. "His future might be to a great extent dependent on the verdict you might return on the question of whether the state of somnambulism, such as this, is considered a state of insanity or not."

In other words, was Fraser to be released, or was he to be put in an asylum?

This was for the jury to decide, but the judge suggested the verdict should be that the prisoner had killed his child when he was unconscious of the act because of his condition of somnambulism: and that the prisoner was not responsible for the act at that time.

The jury accepted this guidance. They did not even retire to deliberate. After briefly conferring among themselves in court, they told the judge through their foreman that they all agreed with the verdict he had suggested, and were pleased to make it their own.

It seemed that Simon Fraser would now walk free, but the prosecutor raised an objection. "In consequence of the verdict," he told the court, "it seems to me that the most advisable course would be to adjourn the case for a short time so that possibly some arrangement can be come to with those who are responsible for the prisoner to see that the public are kept safe."

The judge agreed. Two days later, when the hearing resumed, he announced that the prosecutor had made an arrangement with Fraser and his family as a safeguard against "any possible repetition of such a disaster."

Then, acquitting Simon Fraser, Lord Moncrieff told him he must take every possible step to cure himself of "this unfortunate and involuntary habit" which had already caused him so much misery.

Nobody would say just what had been arranged between the prosecutor, Fraser and his family. But the Frasers' Lime Street neighbours had a good idea. They said it had been agreed that Simon Fraser would sleep alone for the rest of his life, locked in his bedroom by his wife. But by day he would be free.

In an age noted for blind retribution, this was a remarkable victory for compassion and common sense.

Declaration of Simon Fraser 10ᵗʰ April 1878

At Glasgow the tenth day of April eighteen hundred and Seventy eight years In presence of Alexander Carstine Murray Esquire Advocate Sheriff Substitute of Lanarkshire Compeared a prisoner and the charge against him having been read over and explained to him and he having been judicially admonished and examined, Declares and says: My name is Simon Fraser, I am a native of Aberdeen 28 years of age a Sawshafter and I reside at 44 hume Street Glasgow. I have been subject to ~~risings in my sleep~~ since I was ten years old. Last night being my wife and my child / S Fraser

N Euphure Murra~

child Simon Fraser — now deceased an infant not quite 18 months old were in bed in my dwelling house. I dreamt that I saw a white beast flying through the floor and coming to the back of the bed where the child was. I tried ~~to catch at the~~ ~~said beast, and I caught~~ ~~something which I believed~~ ~~to be the beast~~ and I got out of the bed and dashed it on the floor or against the door. I woke up in Consequence of my wife crying and then I found that it was the child I had had in my hands, indeed of a beast, and that the child was very seriously injured.

— S Fraser
A Euphme Murra~

The declaration of Simon Fraser

10

SECRET OF THE WITCH'S MIRROR
LOWER QUINTON, WARWICKSHIRE,
ST. VALENTINE'S DAY, 1945

Witchcraft is still practised in some parts of England.
I could take you to one of them and introduce you to
a witch. So it's hardly surprising that just over half a
century ago, when folk were at least a shade more
superstitious than today, a district of Warwickshire
with a tradition of witchcraft feared the worst when
one of its villagers was found murdered in circumstances strongly suggesting the occult.

The year was 1945, which may not seem that long
ago to anyone over 60, so for a start let us put it into
perspective. When Scotland Yard's Detective Chief
Inspector Robert Fabian — yet to become superintendent — set out to investigate this case in
February, 1945, items carefully packed in his murder
bag included a travelling, unspillable ink bottle.
Ballpoints had yet to arrive. *That's* how long ago it
was ...

He had been summoned to Lower Quinton, a few
miles from Stratford-upon-Avon, to probe the
mysterious and horrifically violent death of 74-year-
old Charles Walton. The elderly widower lived with
his niece in the village of picturesque thatched
cottages and he was still able to earn a bob or two
through his skill at hedging when his rheumatism and

the weather permitted. Both had been favourable on St. Valentine's Day, 1945, so he had set out to see to some hedging on Meon Hill. And the task had cost him his life.

His niece became worried when he didn't come home at his usual time of 4 p.m., but she waited for nearly two hours before she called a neighbour and a local farmer to help her look for him. They knew roughly where he had been working, and it wasn't long before the farmer found him ... and told the niece not to approach.

Charles Walton was not a pretty sight for anyone, least of all a distraught woman. The men turned their torches away, sickened by the spectacle. The old man had been pinned to the ground by his hay-fork, its prongs passing through each side of his neck. His throat and chest had been slashed with his billhook, inflicting deep gashes in the form of a cross, and the murder weapon had been left embedded in one of the wounds. Cuts on his arms showed that he had tried to defend himself, and on his face was a haunting look of sheer terror.

Who could have killed him? Although Charles Walton had been a bit of a crosspatch and had tended to keep himself to himself, he'd had no known enemies. He'd been just a harmless old man going about his work.

Casting around for suspects, Fabian, his partner Detective Sergeant Albert Webb and members of the Warwickshire CID took 4,000 statements from people living in the area, double-checked their accounts of their movements ... and drew a blank. There was a prisoner-of-war camp at Long Marston, a couple of miles away, and Fabian phoned the Yard to obtain the services of a Special Branch detective sergeant who was an accomplished linguist.

The 1,043 prisoners were mostly Italians, and one of them became an instant suspect when he was observed washing blood from his clothes. Furthermore, a baker's roundsman had seen him crouching in a ditch not far from the crime scene, wiping blood from his hands.

The man's coat was sent away for analysis of its bloodstains. Meanwhile sappers of the Royal Engineers had been called in with mine-detectors to sweep the area in a search for the victim's missing tin watch in the hope that it might bear the killer's fingerprints. Now they were directed to search the spot where the Italian had been seen.

Before long the whine of their detectors intensified to a shriek. But instead of the victim's watch they located rabbit-snares. And tests on the suspect's coat revealed only rabbit's blood. The Italian POW had been supplementing his rations through a spot of poaching.

Right from the start Fabian had been conscious that local detectives felt there might be more to the murder than met the eye, but the men from the Yard found it difficult to take their country colleagues' suspicions seriously. Nevertheless, the Warwickshire officers were the investigators who knew the area and its people and their thoughts could not be ignored ... even though they centred on witchcraft!

Warwickshire's Detective Superintendent Alex Spooner, who had called in the Yard, drew Fabian's attention to two accounts of local history. One recorded that in 1875 at Long Compton a young man had killed an old woman whom he believed had bewitched him, despatching her with a hayfork in a manner remarkably similar to the killing of Charles Walton. The other account said that the killer, John Haywood, had sworn he would destroy all 16 of Long

Compton's witches. His *modus operandi* had been a survival of the Anglo-Saxon practice of dealing with witches by spiking them.

Robert Fabian smiled sceptically. Did anyone really expect him to believe, in this day and age, that old Charlie Walton had been killed because he was suspected of witchcraft?

Alex Spooner also smiled, but not quite so sceptically. His smile seemed to say, "Wait and see ..." It wasn't so much that he believed witchcraft was involved. That wasn't the point. He knew the locals and their traditions. He knew how they would react, and what the investigation might be up against.

Fabian himself began to have second thoughts a day or two later when he saw a black dog come running down Meon Hill, followed a moment later by a farm lad.

"Looking for that dog?" the detective called.

"What dog?" asked the boy, hurrying away while Fabian stared after him, mystified. He was to learn that around Lower Quinton black dogs had a significance unattached to their London equivalents.

Spooner filled him in with the story of an Alveston ploughboy's unnerving experience in 1885. The tale had it that on nine successive evenings the boy had encountered a black dog on Meon Hill. On the last occasion the dog turned into a headless woman who rustled past in a black silk dress. And the next day the boy's sister died.

The legend was given a topical twist by the fact that the boy's name was Charles Walton. Could this have been the same Charles Walton whose death was now under investigation? It was possible. Fabian, despite himself, was sufficiently intrigued to make a few inquiries, but whether or not the two were one and the same was never established.

That afternoon a police car ran over a black dog near Meon Hill, on the following day a heifer died for no apparent reason in a ditch, and then a black dog was found hanging by its collar from a tree on the hill.

That was too much for the villagers. They clammed up. They'd had enough of detectives from London stirring up hidden forces that they didn't understand. Fabian himself later recorded that from then on he and his partner got nowhere with their inquiries. The villagers would barely speak to them. Pubs emptied when they walked in.

Although few knew more about murder than Robert Fabian, he had his blind spots. Geography, for instance, was not one of his strong points. He thought Lower Quinton was in the Cotswolds. But although he knew little about witchcraft when he arrived he made it his business to learn more, and by the time he departed he was almost an expert.

One authority on pagan rites expressed no surprise that Charles Walton had died as he did in February. So far as she was concerned, it was to be expected. She explained that traditionally February was a sacrificial month, a time when a human being had to be killed so that his blood replaced the soil's fertility depleted by the previous season's crop. For her Charles Walton's murder was simply a Druidical sacrifice.

Fabian remained sceptical. He had his own ideas about who had murdered Charles Walton, and those suspicions had nothing to do with witchcraft. He became convinced that the killer was none other than Albert Potter, the farmer who had found the body so quickly ... because he knew precisely where to look. And having found it he had grasped the handle of the victim's pitchfork in order, the detective believed, to leave his fingerprints apparently innocently on the implement because they were already on it from a few hours before.

But there was more than this to Fabian's speculation. He had learned that his suspect had a motive. The victim's niece had said that, living frugally, her uncle had always put money aside and by the time of his death he had been a lot better off than most people would have imagined.

The farmer who had found him had been having a difficult time financially, had borrowed money from Charles Walton and had not repaid it, although the elderly hedger had asked for its return.

Furthermore, on his own admission Potter had been the last person known to have seen the victim alive, but his account of his movements contained discrepancies and he kept changing his story.

And Fabian thought that those manifestations of apparent witchcraft — the dead heifer, the hanging dog — had been set up by Potter in order to divert suspicion from himself. It was he who had brought those incidents to people's attention.

So why wasn't he charged? All Fabian had to go on was circumstantial evidence. Although this could often be enough to hang a man, in this case it was not considered sufficient to secure a conviction. So the suspect lived out his days in freedom, eventually to be buried within yards of his victim.

How do we know all this? In his book *The Anatomy of Crime* Fabian wrote: "I have never said this publicly before, but I *think* I know who did it. Who, though, will come forward with the evidence?"

And shortly before he died in 1978 the detective spoke more freely in conversation with the crime-historian Richard Whittington-Egan. The suspect was now dead, Fabian's silence was no longer necessitated by fears of libel, and he named the farmer whom he believed had killed Charles Walton, giving his reasons.

But there were to be other sequels to this strange story. For many years after the murder, on St. Valentine's Day, Meon Hill was visited by Alex Spooner, who would stand quietly, making a point of letting himself be seen.

Years earlier he had expressed his determination to nail the killer. Like Fabian, he had failed. But he must have been aware of the Scotland Yard detective's suspicions, and he now kept his self-imposed annual tryst with Meon Hill to let the suspect know that his guilt was recognised and not forgotten.

Meanwhile in 1960 when land behind Charles Walton's former home was being partially redeveloped, what should turn up but a tin watch found in the debris of what had once been the old man's garden shed?

So had he absent-mindedly left it in the shed on February 14th, 1945? On a day when he would need to know the time because he was out working with no clock in sight, you might think that he would have made a point of taking the watch with him. But then, as a countryman he would have a pretty good idea of the passing of the hours from the position of the sun and the waning of winter daylight.

One man who had known him and his timepiece insisted that the watch which had been found wasn't the one Charles Walton carried. He told Donald McCormick, the author of *Murder by Witchcraft*, that Walton's watch had borne the name of the Stratford-upon-Avon jeweller who sold it, whereas the watch which was discovered had no such inscription.

Then he went on to say something which added to the mystery of the old man, who in his day had attracted some superstitious head-wagging — it was rumoured that he had been seen talking to the birds.

It wasn't Walton's watch, the villager said, because Charlie had always kept a round piece of black glass in the watch-case, and there was no such glass in the watch which had been found.

Why did Charles Walton secrete that piece of glass in his watch-case, and what was its purpose?

The villager said he had wondered that himself and had asked Walton about it on the one and only occasion he had seen it. Charlie had been checking his watch and the piece of black glass had fallen out. But when he was asked what it was for the old man said that was his secret, adding only that it had brought him luck.

The puzzle seemed as inscrutable as the dense black glass itself. Except for one possibility. Black glass has a role in the life of witches. It is known as a witch's mirror...

The village of Lower Quinton
and left, murder victim
Charles Walton

11
THE DARK AGE KILLER
DETROIT, WEDNESDAY, JULY 3RD, 1929

From outside, 3587 St. Aubin Avenue, Detroit, looked much like any other three-storey, timber-framed house on the street. Inside was a different matter. An ornate altar stood in the basement, where the walls were draped with green cloth. Dangling from the ceiling were weird, papier-mâché figures, their grimacing, bestial faces crowned by human hair. And something else also set the house apart on the morning of Wednesday, July 3rd, 1929. It contained six corpses.

The house was the home and office of Beniamino Evangelista, a building and repair contractor, and it was at 10.30 a.m. that day that Ellis Vincent, an estate agent, arrived by appointment.

He mounted the front steps which led almost directly from the pavement, crossed the narrow veranda and rang the doorbell. There was no answer. He rang again and then knocked loudly. There was still no response. This seemed odd because Evangelista was not a man to neglect a business appointment.

Vincent tried the doorknob, opened the door and stepped into the hall, calling the contractor's name. He was met only by silence. He knew that Evangelista's office opened off the hallway to the right. The office door was half open, so he looked in ... and recoiled in horror.

Evangelista's body was slumped in his chair before his desk. His severed head lay on the floor by his feet.

Vincent ran from the house to phone the police. His call was logged at 10.41 and he was asked to remain at the scene until officers arrived. Shortly afterwards, Patrolmen Kennedy Lawrence and Alex Costage found him awaiting them on Evangelista's veranda. Moments later the officers were swallowing hard as they surveyed the scene in the contractor's office. Blood seemed to be everywhere. A crucifix and a reproduction of *The Last Supper* hung on a wall behind the body, and the patrolmen were surprised to see a wig, a beard of false hair and a wooden staff, curiously notched. There were also two swords in the small office, but it was obvious that neither had been used in the decapitation.

"This is for the homicide squad," said Patrolman Lawrence. "I'll go ring them up."

Costage nodded and stood guard at the front door. Shocked neighbours were gathering outside as news spread of the murder. In response to Patrolman Lawrence's call, detectives and uniformed officers arrived, led by Chief of Detectives Edward Fox who spoke first with Ellis Vincent.

"What about the man's family?" he asked. "Anybody else live here with him?"

"Oh, his wife, of course," Vincent answered numbly. "And four young kids."

"Upstairs," Fox ordered his men. They made their way up the staircase, side-stepping bloody footprints indicating a trail to further horror. Fox pushed open the door of the main bedroom. The contractor's wife and infant son lay on the bed. The woman's severed head lay nearby and one of her arms was lacerated at the shoulder as if a hasty amputation had been attempted. Eighteen-month-old Mario Evangelista lay across his mother's other arm. He also had been decapitated.

Stepping gingerly around pools of blood, the detectives went to the adjoining room which contained twin beds. On one lay six-year-old Matilda Evangelista, on the other her younger sister Jenny, aged three. Both had been butchered, their heads cut cleanly from their bodies. On the floor, near the door leading to the upper veranda, lay eight-year-old Angelina. One of her arms displayed a deep cut at the shoulder. A yawning gash in her neck showed that the killer had also meant to behead her.

It seemed that, Angelina excepted, all the victims upstairs had been murdered as they slept. The child who lay on the floor wore a dressing-gown over her nightdress.

"Probably aroused by some sound," Fox commented. "Got up, started for her mother's room, then the killer overtook her. The other victims probably never knew what struck them."

Only Evangelista was fully dressed. At his desk, he had been sitting with his back to the door. He too had probably never known what hit him when he was decapitated by a single blow.

County Medical Examiner Dr. Paul Klebba arrived and viewed the mutilated bodies. He tentatively placed the time of the slaughter between midnight and 3 a.m. The killer, he said, had used a heavy weapon with a cutting edge more than a foot in length — possibly a cavalry sabre, machete or scimitar.

Dr. Klebba also disclosed that the victims actually numbered seven. Evangelista's wife, Santina, was expecting her fifth child.

While detectives were investigating upstairs and conferring with the medical examiner, members of the homicide squad led by Lieutenant John Navarre were going over the rest of the house. Suddenly a detective hurried from the basement. The altar and the room's occult trappings had been discovered.

Inspector Miller, commander of the local police precinct, had known that the contractor was picking up a good income from other activities.

"We'd heard he was head of some kind of cult — faith healing, voodoo, or whatever — but he made no trouble and he had no record," Miller said. "But about a month ago he came around and asked for a permit to hold an exhibition in his house.

"When we asked him to describe the kind of exhibition he had in mind, he talked about it in a queer, confused fashion. So we turned him down on the grounds that it might cause trouble in the neighbourhood. Most of the people around here are extremely devout. We felt they would resent it if Evangelista went in for public exploitation of this cult thing. So I told him, no permit. But it looks like he went ahead with it anyhow."

But what did the Great Celestial Planet Exhibition, which seemed neither celestial nor planetary, have to do with the hideous murders?

It was learned that many who rejected Evangelista's pretensions and paganism respected his powers to cure and heal. One was a neighbour in St. Aubin Avenue who told the investigators: "Some years ago my little Michael was very sick. Somebody told me to take him to Benny, so I did. He read something from a book, it wasn't in English or Italian. He made signs. Then he sat for a long time with his eyes closed. Finally he seemed to wake up. He told us to go home and said my baby would be well again. And right away my little Michael got better."

Detectives also learned of Evangelista's extraordinary courtship, which had won him a charming wife. Photographs of the murdered Santina Evangelista showed a beautiful young woman with the rich olive complexion and dark eyes of her Mediterranean origin.

"She came of a wealthy family in the old country," another neighbour said. "Santina was a very smart girl, but she studied too hard and her health failed. Her father sent her to this country, but still she failed. No one expected her to live. Then Beniamino saw her and he said, 'I can cure this woman. But she must marry me.' "

Santina, the woman went on, had been borne to Evangelista on a stretcher. She seemed willing to accept the cultist's unusual proposal. They were wed immediately, although the bride was unable to rise from her bed. And then came the miracle! The frail bride's recovery to perfect health was the wonder of the neighbourhood.

"Their first-born was that beautiful child, Angelina. And then came the others, all beautiful children, smart, good and healthy," the neighbour recalled.

Seeking further clues, the detectives considered the bloody footprints found in the house. They seemed peculiarly small, almost as small as those of a woman. And yet the killer must have had unusual strength. From the nature of the savage blows and the decapitations, it was also deduced that he was left-handed. Left-handed, enormously strong, but with small, almost effeminate feet! And filled with a brutish hatred for every member of the Evangelista family.

A lead to his identity must lie, the detectives reasoned, in the cult practices of Evangelista. They continued to explore the green room in the basement, investigating masses of documents whose wording was as weird as the suspended images turning and swaying above the strange altar.

Boxes of these papers were removed to police headquarters and examined by Ignace Capizzi, an assistant prosecuting attorney and well versed in Italian. A number of boxes were found to contain trinkets and clothing. Each of these items was tagged with the name of a woman, presumed to have been its former owner.

Capizzi said, however, that it was not to be presumed that the murdered man had given his cult an erotic slant. In certain cults, he said, an accepted ritual involved handling by the miracle man of intimate wearing apparel of a person being sought.

The finding of these articles in Evangelista's basement suggested that he had a side-line as a tracer of lost persons. He had given his cult the lofty title, "The Great Union Federation of America."

Navarre learned that Anthony Evangelista, elder brother of the decapitated cultist, also lived in Detroit, and he was summoned to Fox's office.

"It is a frightful thing, this slaughter of a whole family, even little children," Anthony said. "I am cruelly shocked and grieved. But my brother and I did not come here to Detroit together and I have not seen him more than half a dozen times since I moved here."

"You had quarrelled?" the chief asked.

"Yes — but only in a way to leave pain in the heart, not hatred. I did not wish my brother or his family any ill and I'm sure he felt no lasting bitterness towards me."

"What was the quarrel about?" Navarre asked.

"It was about religion, a real religion and consoling

faith, in contrast to false religion, designed not for faith but for profit."

Anthony explained that the break between the brothers had occurred years ago, in Philadelphia. In 1903, Anthony said, he had been living there and prospering. So he had sent money to pay for the passage of his younger brother to Philadelphia. Beniamino was happy to come to America, but he had some strange ideas.

Anthony, a devout Roman Catholic, was at first bewildered, then outraged by the cult mysticism. After six years, in 1909, the brothers parted company. Beniamino moved to York, Pennsylvania, a region steeped in witchcraft, and stayed there until 1923.

Fox showed Anthony one of the papers he had found among Beniamino's documents. "What do you make of this, Mr. Evangelista?" he asked.

Anthony studied the paper. It was a Black Hand note which had been mailed to Beniamino early in January. It said: "This is your last chance." It was signed: "The Vendetta" and beneath the signature was a crudely drawn hatchet.

Anthony shook his head. "One reads of the Black Hand in the newspapers, but I know nothing of these things. Believe me, I did not behead my brother and his fine family. I was at home with friends during the evening of the second of July, and later asleep in my bed. This I can prove. The shock, the grief of this awful deed is enough." He broke off, wiping his brow.

"You are not a suspect," Chief Fox said. "And thank you for what you have told us."

The detective had gleaned from Anthony Evangelista that the roots of Beniamino's cultist obsession lay not in Michigan but in Pennsylvania. Fox called in two of his best men, Sergeant Dwyer and Detective Roy Pendergrass, and told them to go to Philadelphia and to York.

Meanwhile another relative was waiting to give information. This was Joseph Grillo, a cousin of Mrs. Evangelista.

"I visited the family last Sunday, the 30th," he explained. "I am frequently their guest at Sunday dinner and always Benny is very hospitable, good-humoured and cordial. Last Sunday it was different."

"How different, Mr. Grillo?"

"I noticed it immediately. And I spoke to his wife, Santina, privately about it. Benny was moody, not his usual self. He was usually a great talker. But last Sunday, so silent. A worried man."

"You didn't ask him what was wrong?"

"I was a guest there. And besides, Santina assured me it was nothing. Benny was a busy man and growing rich. He had many moods. This was just one of them. But I felt uncomfortable and I did not stay long."

"You say Evangelista was growing rich?"

"Yes. Benny often treated seventy-five patients in a single day. And he charged as much as ten dollars for each treatment."

This confirmed information already obtained by Lieutenant Navarre who learned that Evangelista supplemented his rites and incantations by prescribing salves and herb concoctions for the sick. He had also built up a flourishing traffic in charms and love potions.

Navarre and Capizzi, from their experience in varied crime cases, were aware that among certain cultists it was held proper to kill the practitioner if the patient died, so a squad of detectives began studying the records of recent deaths, visiting more than a hundred families whose members could conceivably have been among Evangelista's patients.

However, of the families interrogated, only six would even admit having known Evangelista. None of them would admit ever having entered his basement chapel or having applied to him for treatment.

The cultist, the detectives learned, had been too busy with his money-making schemes and property enterprises to bother about being consistent. Although he dispensed "cures" for others, Evangelista had his own family physician who regularly attended his wife and children. And despite his profitable running of a sect he had created, he had remained a regular communicant of a church.

Here he and his family had worshipped and were baptised and here the Evangelistas' funeral was held. Three thousand wedged their way into the church. Others so packed all approaches that police had to keep open a narrow lane to permit the six coffins to be wheeled across from the undertaker's across the street.

Detectives mingled with the throng, looking unsuccessfully for the unknown killer.

In Philadelphia Sergeant Dwyer and Detective Pendergrass learned no more about Evangelista than his brother had already divulged. But in York they questioned old-timers who distinctly remembered the youthful Evangelista.

"All day he works to support himself, but at night and in every spare moment Beniamino preaches," they told the investigators.

In the same Pennsylvania Railroad section gang had been Aurelius Angelino. All the old-timers remembered Angelino. The York authorities, both city and county, also recalled Angelino. Some of them were still looking for him.

Dwyer and Pendergrass noted that Evangelista had moved from Philadelphia to York in 1909. In 1914 Angelino appeared in the "voodoo region" adjacent to the railroad lines which run through the hills between York and Philadelphia. Angelino had come to America from Italy in 1912 with his wife and a son. After their immigration, more little Angelinos were born, a daughter and twin sons.

Angelino and Evangelista were old acquaintances. Both came from the same rural district near Naples. Both had found work as section hands and were neighbours in the same community. Both, moreover, shared the same religious interests.

For years Evangelista had been absorbing the black magic of the area. Undoubtedly the weird rites and tenets of "Great Union Federation of America" were already beginning to evolve. Then, early in 1919, his friend and fellow-mystic Aurelius Angelino went mad. On February 10th he was confined in the Lancaster Insane Asylum. Then on February 17th his wife obtained his release by assuring the authorities that she planned to take her husband back to Italy. But she never got the chance.

The very next day two large milk cans bearing signs "For Sale" were prominently displayed on the lawn in front of Angelino's home. A curious passer-by glanced into one of the cans and drew back with a shocked cry. Inside the can was the dead and mangled body of one of the Angelino twins. The other twin, also mangled, was in the other can.

Dwyer and Pendergrass put in many hours of hard work on the Aurelius Angelino angle. "Angelino was known to be a man of great strength," the sergeant reported to his superiors in Detroit. But after the discovery of the murdered twins, he surrendered without resistance to the police. He tried to claim that he had found his twin boys dead in the cans. But now he was obviously dangerous. So this time they clapped him behind the bars of what was thought a heavy security institution, the Fairview Asylum for the criminally insane. But then on the night of July 16th, 1920, he blackened his face and hands and escaped by impersonating a Negro employee. After being at liberty about one month, he was captured and returned to Fairview. But again, on September 23rd, 1923, he pulled off another escape. And Aurelius Angelino had not again been taken into custody.

The probing by Dwyer and Pendergrass shed new light on Angelino. In 1926, they reported, a man had been killed by a train in a Pennsylvania railroad yard. After his badly mangled corpse had lain unidentified in a morgue for weeks it was viewed and identified by three men who were positive that this was the body of Aurelius Angelino. His widow, wanting to remarry, appealed for a court order that would pronounce her lunatic husband legally dead. This she secured and she remarried at once. The three men turned out to be old friends of Mrs. Angelino.

According to Dwyer and Pendergrass, however, no fingerprints had ever been taken of Aurelius Angelino. Similarly, no fingerprints could be found on file that had belonged to the man who had met his death in the railroad yard. Many Pennsylvania officers consequently suspected that Angelino was still alive and at large.

His friend Evangelista had moved from York to Detroit in 1921, during one of Angelino's periods of incarceration. But the investigators in Detroit failed to establish that Evangelista had seemed to live in dread of an escaped madman after the autumn of 1923. Nevertheless, if Evangelista had not lived in fear of his old pal, he had been living in fear of something during the last months of his life.

Assistant Prosecutor Capizzi had delved into a lot of Black Hand evidence in addition to the threatening note signed "The Vendetta." Evangelista, it appeared, had paid for some form of protection. But he had also acted, at least once, as an intermediary in a transaction that to Capizzi, reading Evangelista's own record of the affair, looked like extortion. Evangelista, as a cultist enriching himself, would be a natural target for extortionists. But apparently he had known how to appease the Black Handers.

Inspector Fred Frahm was convinced that Black Handers had not committed the St. Aubin Avenue murders. "From what I know personally about Black Hand operations," Frahm said, "no Black Hand assassins of recent record have slaughtered an infant or young children, after killing an adult marked for death or retribution."

Evangelista documents being scrutinised by Capizzi and his staff included some of the cultist's own publications. Evangelista had written and published a kind of "bible" entitled "The Oldest History of the World, Discovered by Occult Science." The first words of the preface seemed significant to the investigators because of the time of the massacre fixed by Dr. Klebba, the medical examiner. They were:

"My story is from views and signs that I see from 12 to 3 a.m. It began on February 2nd, 1906, in Philadelphia, Penn., and was completed February 2nd, 1926, in the City of Detroit, County of Wayne, State of Michigan. On this earth the last one created by God the Father Celestial was the great prophet Meil."

Had Evangelista expected his slayer on that night of July 3rd, between midnight and 3 a.m.? Was that why he was dressed and in his office, awaiting the unknown intruder?

One suspect was Umberto Tecchio, one of the last persons known to have seen Evangelista alive. Tecchio was also known to be violent, having fought with his brother-in-law after an argument, knifing and killing him.

Tecchio had been buying a house from Evangelista and it was known that he had taken his wife to visit the cultist for treatment.

"I keep telling you," Umberto Tecchio reiterated under repeated questioning, "I had no motive to kill him, let alone the rest of 'em. I don't know about the weapon. I don't know who would do such a thing."

"But you went to see Evangelista on Tuesday evening, only a few hours before he was killed," said Detective Snyder.

"I went to see Benny, sure, and I had a friend with me. Like I told you, Mike Conti came along. I was only going to give Benny my final payment on that house I've been buying from him. Mike waited outside. Benny and I talked it over. Then I left. It was about eight o'clock."

This would have given Evangelista time to go on an errand the police already knew about, so it seemed as if Tecchio was speaking the truth. On July 2nd, between 8 and 9 p.m. Evangelista had turned up at a location several miles from his home. He was seeking to buy timber to be salvaged from a house being razed. Striking a bargain with the watchman on duty, he had promised to return at 7 a.m. with the purchase price and a truck to haul the wood away. But at 7 a.m. Evangelista was dead.

Though this watchman was the last person known to have seen him alive, he was not considered a suspect. Several people living near the house being razed were positive that he had stayed on his job right through the night.

Detectives questioned Tecchio's companion, Mike Conti.

"Umberto and I live at the same boarding house. It is on Pierce Street and is run by our friend Dominic Giuereato. That Tuesday evening Umberto asked me would I like to walk with him to Evangelista's, as he had some business to attend to. I said okay," Conti told the investigators.

"You and Tecchio went directly to Evangelista's?"

"Yes. It is only a five minute walk. But I did not go in."

"What did you do?"

"I waited on Beniamino's front veranda. Umberto went in. Once or twice I glanced through the window. I saw Beniamino at his desk and Umberto talking to him. I never caught a word that Beniamino said, but I could hear Umberto occasionally."

"Why? Did Tecchio sound angry?"

"He always sounds angry. Ask anyone who knows him. Umberto has a shrill, excited voice, even when asking you the time of day. But I heard no argument and Umberto seemed cheerful when he came out and we walked away. It was then just eight o'clock, I remember. He said that now the house was all his, he'd made his final payment. And he invited me for a drink. Just a round of speak-easies. Tuesday was such a hot, sticky night."

Tecchio and Conti had returned home to Pierce Street by 11 p.m. Conti said he was sure his friend had gone straight to bed since he occupied a room separated from Tecchio only by a curtain.

One of Fox's men had located the artist who had created the images displayed in Evangelista's basement chapel. Those grotesque figures, it turned out, had been made by the foreman of a Detroit decorating company. Questioned at headquarters, the foreman said: "Evangelista gave me rough pencil sketches of the images he wanted. He ordered them to be made 'as horrible as possible.' His very words. I always write down such instructions on the back of the order form."

"What did he say he wanted them for?"

"He said he was going to use them in a lecture tour. Also in a motion picture which he was planning to make."

Capizzi made a further study of the Evangelista "bible" that preached the beliefs of "the great prophet Meil."

Lieutenant Navarre suggested that Evangelista had identified himself with Meil. The notched staff found in Evangelista's bloodstained office was like the one Meil was said to carry. And the number of deep notches in Evangelista's staff matched the number of his children.

To Navarre it seemed that one of Evangelista's disciples or patients had worked up a homicidal frenzy, identifying himself with one of the more uninhibited characters of the cultist's "bible." For through its pages stalked both the righteous and the wicked, all of them addicted to violence.

Prophet Meil's contemporaries believed in decapitation, angered easily and showed their displeasure by slashing or wrenching off limbs. Even cannibalism was on Meil's malignant menu.

"If any Caion men would have knowledge of Aliel women they would be cut to pieces and fed to the hungering slaves."

"And, Chief, it strikes me that whoever nearly amputated Mrs. Evangelista's arm and the arm of little Angelina, had studied this passage." Lieutenant

Navarre showed it to his commanding officer. It read:

"For Trampol had no remorse, for he was a magician. And Berlant began to run away from him, but the blood came out of her shoulder so her power was broken; she cannot magnetise the people any more."

Capizzi, wrestling with the stacks of Evangelista's papers, then found a flat contradiction of the story told by Umberto Tecchio. The property on which Tecchio insisted he had made the final payment was still in Evangelista's name. There hadn't been time for a transfer of title, but Evangelista would have recorded the sale's completion until the business of the deed could be formally concluded. Tecchio was brought in again but he remained defiant.

"Maybe I'm the sucker type," he said. "So what? I'd trusted Beniamino before. I took my wife to him to be fixed up with one of his cures. So why not trust him again? He gives me his word he will write a memo to cover me paying up in full. If I didn't trust his word, I'd have asked Mike Conti to step in and hear him say it."

The investigators suspected that Tecchio had not gone to Evangelista's office that night to pay but to protest.

"What did I have to protest about?" Tecchio countered.

But events had shown that he was not a man to take a fleecing meekly. On April 19th, 1929, just 75 days before the Evangelista murders, Tecchio had fought Bart Maffio over a debt and fatally stabbed him. Bart was his wife's brother and Mrs. Tecchio promptly divorced her husband. The police had shown understanding and accepted Tecchio's excuse that he stabbed his brother-in-law to death in self-defence. Mrs. Tecchio soon married Tony Russo and lived with him in a house that had come to her as part of the divorce settlement. Tecchio widely proclaimed that she had got the house away from him by fraud.

Late in October, 1932, Russo appealed to the Detroit police for protection from Tecchio who, he said, was threatening to blow up the house while Mr. and Mrs. Russo were inside. Shortly afterwards, on November 9th, Tony Russo was shot dead while standing on the veranda of the disputed house. Tecchio, in these circumstances, might have been expected to drop out of sight. But he did not do so. And the violent death of Russo was set down as a suicide.

Then, on Thanksgiving Day, November 29th, 1934, Tecchio's defiance of the police came unceremoniously to an end. He died, it was said, of natural causes. This must have surprised him almost as much as it did those who had managed to survive him. Yet even in death, violence seemed to follow him.

He had lived in the home of Mrs. Mary Henschel who had nursed him during his last illness. But on January 17th, 1935, seven weeks after Tecchio's death, Mrs. Henschel was seen slipping under a railway crossing gate and she was instantly killed by a speeding train.

If Umberto had expired on any day other than Thanksgiving Day, certain persons would have given thanks just the same. And now some of these began to talk. They talked to Detectives Charles Browne and Charles Snyder.

Snyder and Browne had never given up hope of solving the Evangelista case. They had even pursued the investigation in their spare time. And now, late in the winter of 1935, more than five and a half years after the St. Aubin Avenue killings, they were rewarded with facts outranking the scraps of information which had filled the unsolved file since

Patrolmen Lawrence and Costage had first looked down on Evangelista's headless body.

Tecchio's former wife now came forward and confided that she had seen two heavy machetes in Evangelista's office. Neither of these were there when the police examined the murder scene. But Tecchio's ex-wife swore that both she and Tecchio had seen them when they had gone together to Evangelista's when her health needed more of the cultist's incantations.

Browne and Snyder gained another vital fact from young Nick Fricano, who had been only 14 in July, 1929, a newsboy with Tecchio as one of his customers. He said that passing the Evangelistas' home at 5 a.m. that 3rd of July, he had seen Tecchio standing on the front veranda and had spoken to him. Tecchio had answered the newsboy's cheerful greeting with a surly grunt.

The youth had recognised his peril as soon as he learned of the horror that had lain in the Evangelistas' house as he had hurried past it. "I knew enough to be scared of Tecchio," he admitted to the detectives. "Until I knew for sure he was dead, I just kept my lip buttoned up. I wanted to stay alive."

The former Mrs. Tecchio had said much the same thing.

Snyder and Browne located and interviewed some of the men who had lodged at the Pierce Street boarding house when Tecchio lived there. These included his drinking companion Mike Conti and Dominic Giureato, who ran the place. Conti, agreeing that it was now safe to talk, said that he had awoken and noticed that Tecchio was not in his bed. But Conti had considered it unhealthy to reveal this.

Directly after the killings the *Detroit Times* had

offered a $5,000 reward for exclusive information leading to the capture of the Evangelistas' murderer. An additional $1,000 had been offered by Wayne County police departments. But to these potential key witnesses that six-grand offered in the bad Depression year of 1929 had seemed insufficient insurance against the violent and deadly Tecchio.

But despite his appalling record, was Tecchio the type to plot a perfect crime, bringing death to an entire family? To some of the investigators the Evangelistas' slaughter suggested rather the work of some ritual-crazed fanatic.

It suggested Aurelius Angelino.

This deranged religious zealot was capable of the kind of horror wrought in St. Aubin Avenue. He was enormously strong and had proved his guile by escaping repeatedly. And Tecchio didn't have small feet to match the bloodstained footprints. Angelino did — size $5\frac{1}{2}$. And he was remembered in York as a left hander …

Clairvoyants had been called in to assist the investigation, but they had contributed nothing the detectives didn't already know. At one stage it had even been suggested that Evangelista and Angelino were one and the same!

It was left to Chief of Detectives Fox to sum up the investigation, which had got nowhere despite all his efforts. "This is a case," he said, "in which a murderer from the Dark Ages has baffled a thoroughly modernised police force, though every means known to criminological science was employed to detect him."

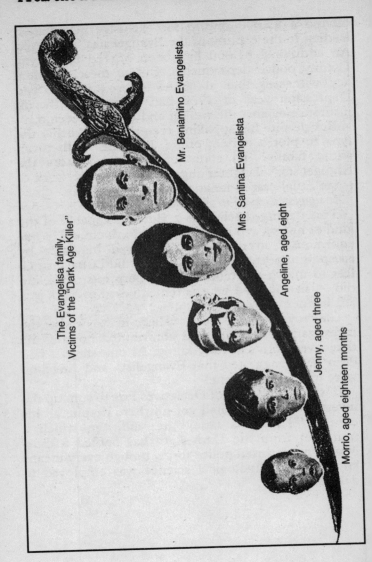

The Evangelisa family.
Victims of the "Dark Age Killer"

Mr. Beniamino Evangelista

Mrs. Santina Evangelista

Angeline, aged eight

Jenny, aged three

Morrio, aged eighteen months

The news of the beheadings spread like wildfire. Crowds outside 3587 St. Aubin Avenue on the morning of the murders

The six coffins at the funeral of the Evangelista family, victims of the "Dark Age Killer"

12
UNDER THE MOST CURIOUS CIRCUMSTANCES
LONDON, JANUARY 25TH, 1932

Real-life coincidences can be stranger than fiction. A passenger on a London bus finds a razor which someone has embedded in one of the rear seats. He takes the razor home and shows it to a friend, who notices that it is stained with blood.

The finder does nothing about his discovery, however, until his friend threatens to report the matter — a London typist's throat has been cut, and newspapers have described the hunt for the weapon, with street drains being searched.

Reluctantly, the finder takes the razor to the police.

Why the delay? The razor's finder has a good job in the City, and he doesn't want to risk jeopardising his position with unfavourable publicity.

So what's wrong with finding a razor and handing it in? Nothing ... except that, coincidentally, some years previously the finder cuts his girl friend's throat with a razor and was imprisoned for wounding, an episode he'd rather forget.

You don't believe this? Well, it happened. The man who found the razor was Kenneth Parsons, an advertising agent. He was on a bus crossing London Bridge on January 30th, 1932, when he made the discovery. When he got off the bus at the Bank of England he didn't report it to the bus conductor, he told a crowded court at the killer's trial, because he didn't want to become involved in any complications arising from his find. So he said nothing and slipped the razor into his pocket.

Recalling the incident in his memoirs, Detective Chief Inspector Ernest Nicholls of the City of London police said: "The discovery of the weapon was made under the most curious circumstances and revealed the most amazing coincidence in my career as a City police officer."

The police hunt for the razor had started days earlier. What led up to it began about two years before that, when a former policeman, Maurice Freedman, made the acquaintance of Miss Annette Friedson, a shorthand typist, who for 10 years had worked for a City of London firm in Fore Street. The two became friends, but Freedman had more than friendship in mind. He borrowed money from the typist, and he told her family they were in love.

Annette's family, however, were uneasy about the relationship. They made inquiries and discovered that Freedman was married. Confronted with this by Annette's shopkeeper father and brother, Freedman said he was seeking a divorce. The Friedsons were not convinced. They asked Freedman to cease seeing Annette.

Freedman consequently stopped calling at the Friedsons' semi-detached villa in Moresby Road, Upper Clapton. But he continued seeing Annette. She made it clear that his attentions were no longer welcome. He responded by phoning her at work every day.

On the evening of Saturday, January 23rd, 1932, the couple had a violent argument. The next day

Annette, in a state of hysteria, told her family that she had finished with Freedman. She also said she was frightened of him.

She was still too upset and nervous to go to work on the Monday, and when she set out for her office the following day her brother accompanied her to her tram, and arranged to meet her outside her office when she left for lunch.

Shortly after 9.30 a.m., a clerk was working in an office in a building opposite the premises of Annette's employers. Looking out of his window, he was startled to see a woman lying on the stairs in the building across the road. Only a few seconds before, he had seen the woman talking to a man. Now he called the police.

Entering the building at about the same time, a book-keeper, Mrs. Clara Bantick, noticed blood on the floor. "It was coming from through the banisters," she said later. "I ran upstairs to the second landing and saw Miss Friedson on her back."

"When I entered the building, I found poor Annette Friedson dead," Detective Chief Inspector Ernest Nicholls recorded in his memoirs. "At 9.26 a.m. she had been seen entering the building, at 9.30 a.m. she breathed her last.

"The whole of her neck had been cut from behind. There were great pools of blood on the stairs and splashes on the walls. She met a most horrible death from a clean-cut wound over six inches long, caused by a razor which had been wielded with great force. After being cut, Annette managed to run up another flight of stairs before she collapsed and died."

It did not take the police long to catch the obvious suspect. Others had seen 36-year-old Maurice Freedman arguing with the 31-year-old typist on the stairs, and they were later able to identify him.

Making off via narrow back streets, Freedman caught a bus at South Place off Moorgate — the conductor remembered him — and went to a cinema.

"He walked about all the night," Nicholls recalled, "and the next morning called on a friend in the Finchley neighbourhood, where I arrested him.

"The night before the crime his landlady had observed him repairing the white handle of an old-fashioned razor which we at first thought had caused the horrible wound. Freedman told me he threw it into a canal in the East End. But he was lying, because the murder was done with a safety razor blade held in a patent attachment ... Some time after the crime, a man walked into the police station and asked to see me. He had with him a bloodstained razor which he said he found on the seat of a bus on the day after the crime ...

"It was the missing weapon. We were able to prove that the blood on the stairs at Fore Street, on Miss Friedson's fur necklet, on Freedman's overcoat and on the razor blade was that of the murdered girl. We found hairs from her fur necklet still clinging to the razor blade."

Investigating Freedman's background, Nicholls found that he had been born in Leeds, where he worked as an errand boy before moving to Birmingham. Joining the army in 1914, he was discharged the following year because of defective eyesight, but he altered his army discharge certificate to show two years' extra service.

He was ordered in 1918 to pay for the maintenance of an illegitimate child, but he made no contribution towards its upkeep.

In the following year he became a Walsall policeman. Three years later he was asked to resign, and two months after that he was married at Birmingham

Registry Office. It was not until after the marriage that his bride found out that he was no longer a policeman. A month later, the couple parted.

First, Freedman worked as a travelling salesman. Then he became a barman at the Red Lion in Finchley, subsequently taking a job as a doorman at the Poplar Pavilion Cinema and the Poplar Hippodrome. Sacked because of his rudeness to patrons, he took out a pedlar's licence and claimed he earned a living by selling brushes from door to door. Nicholls, however, suspected that he never did any peddling.

Freedman had obtained £75 by false pretences from a customer at the pub where he had worked for two years, and he borrowed £50 from Annette — a record of some of the amounts she had lent him was found in her handbag. He had told her he was in partnership with a bookmaker. The only truth in this was that most of the money Annette lent him had been lost in betting.

At the time of his arrest, when he was living in Oakfield Road, Clapton, his possessions amounted to little more than a collection of pawn tickets in false names, pledging his clothes and boots. Instead of underpants, he was wearing some old pyjama trousers.

Nevertheless, he wore a new pin-stripe suit for his Old Bailey trial before Mr. Justice Hawke in March, 1932.

Tall and spruce, with his hair slicked back, and wearing black-rimmed spectacles, he was described by Nicholls as "the coolest murderer who ever stood in the dock at the Old Bailey."

Sir Percival Clarke KC, prosecuting, had a reputation for ruthless cross-examination, but Freedman's composure remained unruffled — as if, Nicholls commented, he had not a single care in the world.

After taking the oath in the Hebrew manner with his hat on, he told the court: "On the morning of the tragedy I did not go out to kill Annette Friedson. I did not know I had the white-handled razor in my pocket.

"When I met her at the door of her office I said 'Hullo, Ann,' and she handed me my fountain pen and my mother's photograph.

"She said she had told them at home that she would not see me again. As we went up the stairs, I said, 'Don't leave me. You know we love one another. You know I shall do something to myself.'

"I was standing below her, and I took the razor from my pocket, opened it, and showed it in the hope that she might change her mind.

"I put it towards my throat, and she took hold of my hand and pulled. There was a struggle, and I saw her fall. I became afraid and bewildered and ran down back streets to the Bank, where I got on a bus."

He said he went to a cinema in Finsbury Park, staying there until it closed at 10.45 p.m. Then he walked the streets and rested at an all-night café in Hampstead Road.

The conductor of the bus on which the razor was found stuffed into the back seat on the upper deck, told the court that he remembered Freedman occupying that seat on the bus. The passenger had appeared agitated, and sat in an unusual way, with his knee near the bell-push.

The police alleged that when Freedman was arrested he said, "Don't hold me. I am the man you are after. I admit cutting the gir'' throat in the City and will give you no trouble. I have been walking about all night, am fed up, and was going to give myself up for the job."

When Freedman was charged, however, he said: "I

don't admit cutting the girl's throat," and at his trial he repeated this denial.

Unimpressed by Freedman's claim that Annette Friedson had died accidentally in the struggle for the razor, the jury found him guilty of her murder, and he was sentenced to death.

Maurice Freedman's appeal was subsequently rejected, and Detective Chief Inspector Nicholls recalled, "A month later I went to Pentonville Prison and identified his dead body after the executioner had cut him down from the scaffold. Never in my career did I gaze upon the corpse of such a worthless fellow."

From the X Files of Murder

The murder weapon — a razor
blade in a patent holder

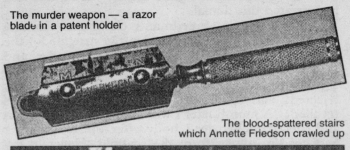

The blood-spattered stairs
which Annette Friedson crawled up

Bloodstained walls where Miss Friedson was first attacked

13
KILLING FIELDS OF THE DEVIL WORSHIPPERS
MATAMOROS, MEXICO, MARCH 14TH, 1989

A year ago Mark Kilroy had made a promise. Now, in 1989, he was keeping it. The 21-year-old student from Santa Fe, Texas, had returned to Mexico just as he said he would, to attend the spring festivities. He and three friends had come to the Mexican border city of Matamoros. They mingled with the fun-loving, carousing crowds that thronged the streets in the early hours of Tuesday, March 14th.

The spring night had been one of bar-jumping in the Mexican city, of loud talk and laughing, of blaring music from the street cantinas, flashing-eyed señoritas and purveyors offering for sale anything under the sun.

But shortly before 2 a.m. Mark, a handsome blond youth heading for the international bridge to return to American soil, became separated from his companions. When they looked around for him he was nowhere to be seen.

They thought he would show up shortly, probably to report embellishments to the night of fun and games.

But as the sobering effect of the next few hours set in the seriousness of the situation became apparent.

The worried college friends sought the help of U.S. Customs authorities after crossing the Gateway International Bridge into Brownsville. There, Oran Neck, special agent in charge of the U.S. Customs Service investigations office, listened to their story of Kilroy's disappearance from the Matamoros street and launched a hunt. Customs Service agents accompanied the three youths back to the Mexican border city to retrace their steps.

It was possible that the youth had ended up in a Mexican jail — not an uncommon occurrence for festive-minded tourists. The investigators combed the city's prisons and police stations. Mexican authorities co-operated in the search, but nothing turned up on Kilroy's whereabouts.

Kilroy's friends notified his parents in Santa Fe, who said they would come to Brownsville and Matamoros to help in the search. They knew that Mark would not have voluntarily absented himself for long.

Fear of foul play was now uppermost in the minds of the searchers. They wondered if Mark had somehow fallen victim to border violence precipitated by drug-trafficking.

In November, 1988, a Texas man and his wife had been fired on by snipers on the Mexican side of the Rio Grande as the couple rafted down the river. The man had been killed and his wife, though badly wounded, escaped to notify the authorities. The snipers were eventually caught and admitted they had been high on drugs. Then on March 29th and April 1st that year the bodies of nine men and three women had been found in a well and sewage pit tank at an abandoned ranch near Agua Prieta, Mexico. The victims had been tied up, tortured and shot to death. All were Mexican nationals. The dozen murders were thought to be connected to slayings, two days earlier, of five men whose bound and stabbed bodies were found stacked in a shed in a rented home in Tucson, Arizona. Officers there said that the five murders were also drug-related.

On April 27th, 1989, the prime suspect in the drug murders, a Mexican who owned the ranch where the bodies were found was arrested and turned over to the Mexican authorities.

Mexican officials said he was charged with first-degree murder, concealment of accomplices, criminal association and violation of burial laws. Still another body possibly linked to the Agua Prieta and Tucson drug murders had been found several days earlier by police in Sonora, Mexico. The corpse, identified as that of a reputed Mexican drug dealer, was found five miles south of Agua Prieta. The victim had been shot twice in the back of the head. His arms were tied behind his back and lime had been tossed on the body, as was the case in the other killings.

Besides the series of murders stemming from drug-trafficking, robbery-killings are a frequent occurrence in the border cities.

Such slayings are mostly of illegal aliens crossing or trying to cross into the U.S., but it wasn't possible that such a fate could have befallen an innocent tourist like Mark Kilroy.

His relatives and friends walked around Matamoros putting up posters that offered a reward for information leading to his safe return, but days, then weeks, passed with no results.

As a last resort, investigators arranged to have one of the friends who had been with Mark placed under hypnosis. They hoped this might yield a clue from his subconscious.

The hypnosis produced the first tangible piece of

information on the mysterious disappearance. While under, Mark's friend remembered something that had happened before the group noticed Mark was no longer with them.

He recalled he had glimpsed a man, an Hispanic, motion to Mark and say something. This had happened near a café just a few yards from the international bridge. From his deep subconscious, the friend recalled that the man had been wearing a blue plaid shirt and had a cut or a scar on one cheek. He had spoken to Mark in English.

As best the friend could recall, the man had said to Mark. "Hey, don't I know you from somewhere?"

Mark had stopped, apparently to talk with the stranger. After that the friend remembered nothing else, except that it was the last time they had seen Mark.

No ransom demands had been made since his disappearance, so if he had been abducted and robbed it was possible that he had been slain and dumped.

More than 100 people were quizzed by the authorities on both sides of the Rio Grande, but no leads developed.

In Brownsville, Cameron County sheriff Alex Perez put Lieutenant George Gavito in charge of the investigation. Gavito was convinced that the student had met with foul play and was probably dead. He enlisted the help of the Border Patrol to comb the Rio Grande and its banks. Helicopters and four-wheel-drive vehicles that could plough through the deep sand of the area were summoned, but failed to find anything.

As the hunt went on, Mexican police were also waging their continuing battle with drug smugglers. No one, even the veteran officers who had seen all kinds of violence and death in their border work, could have anticipated the stark horror that would be uncovered during what was thought to be a routine drug-trafficking investigation.

On Sunday, April 9th, the driver of a truck crashed through a roadblock for drug smugglers that was manned by Mexican police. The driver seemed oblivious to the block as he drove through at high speed.

Pursuit of the lorry led the Mexican officers to a small ranch about 16 miles west of Matamoros, and when investigators searched the vehicle they found a quantity of marijuana. Suspecting that the ranch and its scattered assortment of rundown shacks was the base for a border drug smuggling operation, the police obtained a search warrant to go over the premises. When they descended on the site they arrested two suspects.

Their search turned up about 100 pounds of marijuana, some cocaine and a cache of arms including machine guns. But what was to prove more significant was stark evidence that members of the group practised voodoo or black magic in a dilapidated shack.

Among the suspects rounded up after the Sunday raid was the caretaker of the ranch. During interrogation he spoke of strange happenings in the shack near the main ranch house, saying he was once ordered not to come close.

On a hunch, an investigator showed him a photograph of Mark Kilroy. The caretaker glanced at the picture and said that he had seen him, handcuffed, in a vehicle at the ranch a few weeks earlier.

The Mexican police arrested two more men the next day and questioned them at length. Commandante Juan Ayala, who had been cracking down hard on Mexican drug operations since being assigned to the border post, notified the Brownsville Sheriff's Department of the big break in the Kilroy case. At daybreak the Mexican and Cameron County officers, along with U.S. Customs agents headed by Perez, converged on the site known as Rancho Santa Elena.

They had with them the suspects, whom the Mexican police said had confessed to being involved in two killings at the ranch — one of them of the missing Mark Kilroy.

When they arrived at the ranch the officers expected to find two bodies. The suspects in custody had admitted killing Kilroy after abducting him from a Matamoros street. They also disclosed the murder of another victim.

Their motives reeked of fire and brimstone. They said they were devil-worshippers, members of a cult who believed they would have lasting immunity from detection and arrest for their drug smuggling operations if they offered up human sacrifices. They claimed to have performed sickening rituals in the weathered shack on the Rancho Santa Elena.

The cult members believed so strongly in the black magic they practised that they were sure they were invisible to the human eye. That explained why the man who had driven through the police blockade on Sunday had been so confident. He had thought the police couldn't see him or his truck!

The excavation for evidence started on the lonely ranch at 6 a.m. One suspect first directed officers to a spot which he said concealed the remains of Mark Kilroy. Customs Agent Neck saw a chain sticking from the ground, and when the site was dug up it became clear that the chain protruding from the ground was attached to the spinal cord of the victim.

The suspects said they had planned to pull out the backbone after decomposition so they could use the vertebra to make necklaces.

Instead of finding two graves, the officers looked on in amazement as the suspects guided them to yet more graves of young males.

"There, and there, and over there," said one of the suspects, gesturing.

As sunshine replaced the dawn's greyness, the air grew fetid as the mass disinterments continued. Four graves were within a rough, wooden-fenced corral about 40 feet from the shack where the victims were said to have been slain. Other burial sites were scattered around the corral area.

One grave contained two bodies, another held three, and seven were in single graves about six feet apart.

More gruesome details of the murders came to light as bodies removed from the shallow graves showed evidence of torture and mutilation. Some victims had been shot in the head, others had apparently been struck on the head with a sharp instrument. The ritualistic killings had taken place in the shack about half a mile from the main ranch house.

Four cauldrons contained a dried chicken head, gold-coloured beads in oil, and a goat's head. Wooden sticks had been jammed into a vile, sloppy mixture in the largest two-foot-wide cauldron. Investigators identified the evil-smelling contents as animal bones, human blood and human brain matter. Inside the shack the air was foul with strange odours.

The building contained the remains of a kind of altar, littered with candles, broken glass, cigar butts, chilis and bottles of cane liquor.

The suspects said these were offerings to their

devil-gods. As the exhumations and the gathering of the grisly evidence continued, officers listened in shocked silence as the four Mexican suspects coolly related details of their activities.

One of the suspects talked freely about Kilroy's abduction and killing, making a full statement to the Mexican authorities.

The probe revealed that Mark Kilroy had been a prisoner in a barn for about 12 hours before being slain. It was also discovered that he had been picked at random. Most of the other victims had also been randomly selected, except two who had been killed because they had ripped off the devil-worshippers.

While held captive in the barn, Kilroy had been fed raw eggs. His arms had been bound behind him and his mouth taped. He had been killed in the murder shack by a blow from a machete to the back of the head, his brain removed and the chain attached to his spine before his body was buried. One suspect explained that Mark's legs had been severed so the body would fit into the grave.

The full horror of the devil-worshipping rituals came to light when the investigators learned that one victim had been boiled alive and another decapitated and castrated.

They had apparently been killed on a bloodstained tarpaulin found on the earthen floor of the shack. Pennies were found in one of the cauldrons. The suspects told investigators that they worshipped over these, hoping to make a lot of money in their drug operations.

According to the officers on the case, the cult members had been conducting human sacrifices for about nine months. Investigator Gavito said: "They prayed to the devil that the police would not arrest them, that bullets would not kill them, and that they would make more money."

The Mexican authorities ordered autopsies on the victims. With the exception of Kilroy and another man from Texas, the other murder victims were Mexican nationals, all young men. The cult suspects in custody said that they did not kill females.

They provided the names of half a dozen other gang members, including the identity of two of the cult's ring-leaders.

Adolfo de Jesus Constanzo, 26, was named as the spiritual leader and chief executioner for the devil cult. A U. S. citizen, he was known as the *padrino*, the godfather, and was assisted in running the organisation and life-taking rituals by a young woman, Sara Maria Aldrete, 24. She was known to the cult members as the *bruja*, or the witch. Though a native of Mexico, the tall, striking "witch woman" was a student at Texas Southmost College, Brownsville. As the investigation progressed it was learned that she had a dual personality and led a Jekyll-and-Hyde existence. When it was unravelled in the next few days it shocked her family, friends and tutors.

The godfather and witch woman disappeared at about the same time that the federals raided the ranch. Constanzo, the officers discovered, was a charismatic figure who had properties in Miami and Mexico City and moved in circles which included media celebrities, political figures and the elite of the drug-trafficking underworld on both sides of the border.

It had been the godfather who killed Mark Kilroy, the cult suspects told the officers. Earlier he had ordered them to abduct any male American from the revellers. The victim's sacrificial death would protect the smugglers from American police, the godfather had said.

In Brownsville the sheriff's department issued an all-points bulletin for Constanzo and Sara Aldrete on charges of aggravated kidnapping in the snatching of Kilroy. It was reported that the couple might be heading for Miami and the authorities there were alerted. Similar orders were also issued for the other cult members named by the men in custody.

Meanwhile Mexican police searched the Matamoros residence of Sara Aldrete, where she lived in an upstairs apartment in the home of relatives. There the police found an altar, assorted cult objects including candles, and blood spattered on the wall. So had the girl performed killing rituals in the apartment in the fashionable Matamoros neighbourhood too?

Her relatives were stunned by the findings. They professed no prior knowledge that she had been involved in devil-worshipping rites, but they had to believe it all now.

As the manhunt for the two cult leaders spread over Mexico and the United States, developments were breaking fast on the murder ranch. One of the suspects was taken back to the site to dig up still another body that he said was buried in the killing field.

The suspect was handed a pick and shovel. He proceeded to work in the broiling midday sun. After a while a portion of the corpse came into view, and the cloying stench of rotting flesh hung in the air, prompting the suspect to request a face mask to complete the job.

"You didn't need one when you buried him," a Mexican officer growled.

The suspect dug until the body of a man thought to be in his 30s was recovered. It became quickly apparent that like other corpses found on the death ranch, this body had been cut open and the heart removed.

With the disinterment of the 13th body, the Mexican and Texas authorities arranged for bulldozers and other equipment to start excavating the ranch.

Police then revealed that blood-spattered clothing belonging to children had been found in Sara Aldrete's apartment. They now feared that children might also have been victims of the satanic rituals, but the suspect who had dug up the latest body said no children had been discovered. He said the bloody clothes found in the woman's apartment belonged to one of Sara's relatives. The blood must have come from another source, because the boy who owned the clothes was alive and uninjured, he said. This was verified by the police.

The investigators heard that Constanzo and Sara Aldrete had last been seen together in a silver or blue Mercedes-Benz. No one was sure whether they were still travelling together.

In a co-operative probe between the U.S. and Mexican law enforcement agencies, a profile of the handsome Constanzo began to take shape. A Cuban-American born and raised in Miami, where his refugee family had settled, he had left in the mid-1980s for Mexico City. He was said to travel between there and Matamoros at least once a week to oversee the drug-smuggling operations and the hocus-pocus that the cult members believed made them invincible. The so-called godfather had performed his devilish work in return for half of the gang's vast profits.

Lieutenant Gavito said that Constanzo was extremely wealthy. The fact that he had bought the brand-new Mercedes for cash said it all. He had also paid cash for other luxuries, including jewellery and fur coats.

"He had out-of-body experiences, healing the sick and predicting the future," said a relative who had known the cult leader as a boy. Although he had dropped out of school, he'd had two things going for him — his uncanny psychic talents and his good looks. This combination of looks, psychic abilities and charm coupled with sophistication put him in touch with Mexico City's high society. People paid him thousands of dollars for his fortune-telling and ritualistic "cleansings."

It was reported that his customers included top-ranking government officials and some of Mexico's most popular entertainers — all of whom would later deny any link with Constanzo.

It was not known how Adolfo Constanzo met Sara Aldrete, but somewhere along the way their paths crossed, setting the stage for drug-smuggling and devil-cult rituals.

Sarah drew stares wherever she went. She was 6 feet 1 inch tall, had light brown hair and striking features. She was bright and sparkling and popular at college. Born in Matamoros, she had grown up in a middle-class neighbourhood and enrolled at the Brownsville college in 1986.

She was among 30 people added to the school's "Who's Who" list in 1988 and had been named as the outstanding physical education student. One of her professors, on hearing of her spiritual exploits said, "This is totally unbelievable. She never showed any signs of unusual behaviour. She was always cheerful, always well-groomed and dressed, a model student and a striking woman."

But Lieutenant Gavito said, "It looks to us like she was leading a double life. She had one life in Matamoros. Her friends here didn't know what her life was in Mexico."

Investigators quizzed other students who had seen a darker side to her personality. One of them recalled that she and Sara had once watched a videotape of a TV documentary about Caribbean voodoo rites known as Santeria. She remembered that while they talked about the videotape Sara had asked, "Do you want to know what Santeria is?"

"Then she told us about the rituals they had — she told us they covered themselves in blood to purify themselves. By the time she had finished, we knew she knew what she was talking about and we were scared. She kind of hinted that she was one of a very few chosen ones who lead such cults."

Another friend said Sara had never mentioned human sacrifices, but the investigators had a theory that Sara, as the high priestess of the drug cult, had lured men across the Rio Grande so that the gang could abduct and murder them. At least one of the suspects in custody had said that it was Sara who used her charms to induce him to join the group.

Long before the devil cult's killing activities came to light, drug agents on both sides of the border were aware of the marijuana-smuggling operations by gangs whose members had once been poor farmers. It wasn't surprising that those farmers came to the conclusion that there was a bonanza in smuggling marijuana up north. There seemed to be an unlimited demand.

The operations of one particular family was considered small-time by the authorities. It was within this gang, a family that suffered a violent split wrought by rivalry over drugs profits, that the devil cult rituals had their demonic birth.

The feud had led some family members to turn to black magic. Things began to fall apart for the dope-smuggling gang when its 38-year-old chieftain was gunned down on a Matamoros street in January, 1987. After that the others lacked connections, power and money.

In the spring of 1988 one of the family who had heard about Adolfo Constanzo went to Mexico City and offered him a deal — half of all profits if he could come through with supernatural protection.

Constanzo was more than willing to trade his devilish influence for dope money. Sara Aldrete became the priestess of the outfit, using her intelligence and charm to recruit gang members and lure potential victims into the web.

Though she apparently hadn't taken part in the sacrificial rites, she had helped set the stage for violent ceremonies by showing a video of *The Believers*, a 1987 film that depicted wealthy Americans resorting to human sacrifices to protect their prominence.

As the authorities continued to amass a thick file on the dope smugglers, the body count rose again. Investigators followed up a tip by children who said they had seen a hand sticking from the ground on another ranch, the Rancho Los Leones, that belonged to other members of the family.

Mexican police dug in a clearing in an orchard and discovered a grave containing the bodies of two unidentified males. Later the remains were identified as those of two suspected drug-traffickers, one a 52-year-old Texan, the other a Mexican who lived on a small farm near Matamoros. Neither appeared to have been tortured or mutilated.

The investigators believed that the two victims had been involved in the operations of the drug-cult gang led by Constanzo. In Brownsville, Sheriff Perez told newsmen that the two newly discovered murders were "drug-related, revenge-type killings."

Meanwhile, eight of the 13 victims on the other ranch had been identified. Five others were buried in paupers' graves, their identities unknown. In a Catholic church near Santa Fe, Mark Kilroy was laid to rest. An estimated 1,000 mourners attended the service.

In Matamoros, families of missing relatives seeking to identify the victims filed through a funeral home where the bodies had been taken.

It was unlikely that the remains could be recognised because of the advanced state of decomposition, but a forensic specialist had performed autopsies on seven of the corpses and reported that in addition to the castrations, the men's lungs, hearts and brains had been removed. In several cases the skin had been peeled from their faces. Some of the mutilations had been carried out while the victims were alive.

In addition to Kilroy, those said to have been identified included Gilberto Garza Soa, about 36; Victor Saul Sauceda-Galvan, a 22-year-old policeman; and Valente Del Fierro. Additional victims included Jose Garcia, 14; Ezequiel Rodriguez Lana, 27; Ruben Vela Garza, 30; and Ernesto Rivas Diaz, 23 — all from Mexico.

Police told newsmen that three of the victims identified as drug-traffickers — Luna, Garza and Diaz — had been machine-gunned to death by Constanzo.

The two bodies found on the other ranch were identified as Moises Castillo of Houston, and Hector de la Fuente, 39, who lived near Matamoros.

Meanwhile in Mexico City, several hundred miles from where the mass murders had been unearthed, police were hot on the trail of Constanzo and his towering priestess Sara Aldrete.

Officers swept down on two houses where Constanzo was known to have lived. One was a place that the cult leader maintained in the capital city. The other was a large white stucco house 11 miles from the city centre.

The first house yielded names and addresses of other cult members, as well as a photograph of Adolfo Constanzo. Inside the heavily guarded stucco house police discovered the cult leader's version of a Santeria altar. Armed federal agents raided the large house but found that Constanzo had left earlier. Neighbours said that several young men who claimed to be university students had moved into the house two years before.

Inside, officers found the remains of goats and chickens. The animals had apparently been used for sacrifices. According to neighbours, the "students" usually dressed in black and drove large luxury cars with foreign licence plates.

As the manhunt continued, agents learned that Constanzo had ties in Houston, Texas, and had purchased luxury cars there.

Mexican officials speculated that Sara Aldrete might be dead, a murder victim herself. There were reports that her passport and handbag had been found in the white stucco house in Mexico City. There was one theory that she had been slain by Constanzo to keep her quiet. It was learned that he and three other men had boarded a flight from Brownsville to Mexico City on April 11th, the day the bodies had been discovered on the Matamoros ranch.

Address books found in the big stucco hideaway prompted police to question men in Mexico City's homosexual community, where the cult leader was said to be well known.

"They are men who knew him from parties and

gay bars," a Mexican investigator said. He added that pornographic magazines showing men engaged in sex acts were found in Constanzo's apartment. Investigators also turned up a photo of Constanzo with a man they said was his lover.

The suspects in custody continued to spill what they knew about the cult leader: he drank alcohol but didn't use drugs, and he forbade their use by any of the gang. Police confirmed that he had slain one member for using cocaine.

The authorities were deluged with scores of tips about "sightings" of Constanzo and Aldrete and other cult members.

In the central part of Mexico City residents of one neighbourhood wondered about the occupants of an old apartment building. The residents seemed to be preoccupied with keeping their activities secret. When they bought large supplies of groceries they made it a point to lug home the groceries themselves and not allow any delivery people into their apartment. And there was the strangely behaved, tall woman with the man, who increased the curiosity of the neighbours. Finally somebody went to the police and told them of their suspicions.

As a result, on Saturday, May 6th, 1989, officers combed a five-block area around a supermarket looking for the suspects. They spotted a black Chrysler which was thought to belong to the elusive cult leader. They were looking at the car when a burst of gunfire broke out from a fourth-floor window of a nearby apartment building.

As the armed officers scurried for cover and began returning the gunfire, someone began throwing handfuls of paper money from the apartment window. A man who scuttled about trying to gather some was wounded in the blaze of shots being fired.

Some 45 minutes later, after reinforcements wearing bulletproof vests had swarmed into the area, the officers stormed the apartment. As they burst through the door the people inside surrendered. The officers looked into a closet and discovered the bullet-riddled bodies of two men.

The survivors of the gun battle said that the bodies were those of Adolfo Constanzo and his male lover, Martin Quintana Rodriguez, who was reputed to have been the godfather's right-hand man. Unbelievable though the story sounded, the suspects claimed that Constanzo had ordered them to kill him and Rodriguez after the gunfight with police broke out.

Among those arrested was Sara Aldrete. She had cut and dyed her hair to avoid identification, and she too said that one of the gang members, Alvaro de Leon Valdez, had been ordered by Constanzo to kill him and his companion, Rodriguez. This was confirmed by de Leon Valdez in his statements to police and reporters.

He said that he had been asleep when Constanzo spotted the officers and mistakenly thought their hideout had been pinpointed.

The suspect said that after one member shouted that the police were there Constanzo had gone berserk. "Then he grabbed a bundle of money and threw it out of the window. He said if he could not enjoy the money, no one else could either."

As police ringed the apartment, the cult leader had begged de Leon Valdez to kill him and his male lover, the suspect said. As de Leon Valdez baulked, Constanzo told him it would be hard on him in hell if he didn't comply with the order.

The suspect said, "He slapped me twice in the face. We could hear the cops outside shooting. A lot of shots could be heard. They sat down in a cupboard, Constanzo on a stool and Martin beside him. I just stood there in front of them and pulled the trigger. That was it."

He had riddled then with a Uzi machine-gun, according to his story. He said he had continued shooting through the window at the police until his ammunition ran out.

Valdez admitted having taken part in several of the killings on the Matamoros ranch and said that he and others had sat around a table watching Constanzo mutilate the victims. Also arrested in the apartment were a man and a woman identified as Omar Ochoa and Maria Rofillo Gomez. Police said two had escaped during the battle.

At first the U.S. authorities suspected that Constanzo might have faked his death and had someone else killed by the machine-gunner, but the cult leader was positively identified by his fingerprints.

Mexican authorities booked the suspects on charges of homicide, criminal association, wounding a police officer during the arrest, and damage to property.

On May 9th Mexican officials announced that the drug-cult gang had apparently been involved in eight other slayings that had occurred in 1987 in Mexico City and were similar to the Matamoros ritual killings.

Police said the victims included five men and three women whose mutilated bodies were found at the bottom of a lake. The corpses were discovered after a tip that a housekeeper had disappeared after telling friends she planned to attend a black mass.

The victims' chests had been cut open and their bodies mutilated, said the police. The bodies were bound to cement blocks with wire.

"These cases were very definitely linked to Constanzo," said Rodrigo Martinez, chief of the team probing the slayings.

The five captured in the apartment shootout were later indicted in a Mexican court on charges of murder and related charges in the slaying of Constanzo and Rodriguez. The Mexico City suspects were not charged in the Matamoros ranch killings.

Sara Aldrete denied involvement in any of the killings, though Mexican prosecutors said she had made statements implicating her in the gang's operations. The cult members were also charged in Texas with drug-smuggling.

The case left open one disturbing question that would never be answered: how many more victims would the devil-worshippers have claimed but for the investigation of Mark Kilroy's disappearance?

Sara Aldrete

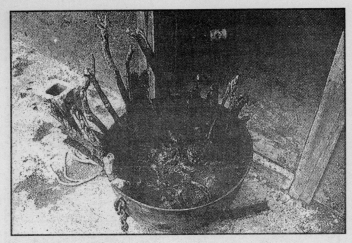

Sticks rammed into a cauldron of bones, blood and brain matter

Deputies dig
for bodies at
the Rancho
Santa Elena

Murder shack on the ranch of horror. The cauldron can be seen in doorway

Adolfo Constanzo